THREE HORSES

by Erri De Luca

Translated by Michael F. Moore

Other Press · New York

This book was originally published as TRE CAVALLI © 1999 by Giangiacomo Feltrinelli Editore, Rome, Italy.

The publication of this book has been made possible thanks to a translation grant offered by the Italian Ministry of Foreign Affairs.

Translator copyright © 2005 Michael F. Moore

Production Editor: Mira S. Park
Book design by Kaoru Tamura

This book was set in 11 pt. Garamond by Alpha Graphics of Pittsfield, NH.

10 9 8 7 6 5 4 3 2 1

Library of Congress Cataloging-in-Publication Data

De Luca, Erri, 1950-
[Tre cavalli. English]
Three horses / by Erri De Luca ; translated by Michael F. Moore.
   p. cm.
ISBN 1-59051-135-2 (pbk. : alk. paper)
I. Moore, Michael F. II. Title.

PQ4864.E5498T7313 2005
853'.914—dc22

2004021061

FOREWORD

Argentina is a right triangle. The Andes to the west make its vertical leg. The jagged line of the rivers to the north make its horizontal leg. The Atlantic Ocean to the east, its corroded hypotenuse.

Argentina is three thousand, seven hundred kilometers long, and lies between the twenty-first and fifty-third parallels of the Southern latitude. The last clod of American soil, shared with Chile, is only ten degrees away from Graham Land, the horn of the Antarctic continent.

Argentina welcomed about seven million emigrants to its shores before 1939. Almost half of them were Italian.

From 1976 to 1982 Argentina suffered under a military dictatorship that decimated a generation. By the end almost forty thousand people were missing. Almost all of them were young and never received a burial.

The dictatorship collapsed after the failed invasion of the Falkland/Malvinas Islands, half the size of Sicily, more than three hundred kilometers from the coast. It was the spring of 1982.

This immensity of places and events is connected to the accidents that befell people in this story.

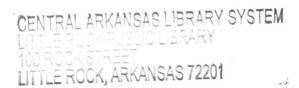

Castigo para los que no practican su purezza con ferocidad.

Woe to those who do not practice their purity ferociously.

—MARIO TREJO, *Argentina 1926*

I ONLY READ USED books.

I lean them up against the bread basket, turn the pages with one finger, and they stay in place, so I can chew and read at the same time.

New books are petulant. The pages don't stay down after you turn them. They resist and you have to press them flat. Used books have loose bindings. The pages go by without springing back up.

So when I go to the tavern at noon, I sit in the same chair, ask for a soup and some wine, and read. Novels of the sea or mountain adventures—never stories of the city, which already surround me.

I look up when a glint of the sun reflects off the windowpane in the door. Two people come in, she wearing a hint of the wind, he a hint of ash.

I go back to my book about the sea: a storm is brewing, force eight; the young man is eating heartily while his mates lose their lunches. Then he goes out on the bridge to stand tall because he's young, alone, and exhilarated by the storm.

I look up to sprinkle some raw garlic in my soup. I swallow a spoonful of something bitter, gnarly and red.

I turn docile pages, slow morsels, then I tear my head away from the white of the paper and the tablecloth and follow the line formed by the upper edge of the wall tiles in its tour around the room, passing behind the two black pupils of a woman, which sit on the vector like two notes split apart by the lower line of the pentagram. They're staring straight at me.

I raise my glass to the same point and hold it steady before drinking. The alignment etches the beginnings of a smile in my cheeks. The geometry of the things around us creates coincidences, intersections.

The woman smiles openly.

From behind her the man intercepts the toast and begins to twist his torso, leading with his elbow. The host dodges him with a shift of the hips while carrying a plate to me. Before the dynamo completes his half-turn I bark out a greeting to the woman as if I know her. She responds in kind while the man glares at me.

I continue drinking and go back to my plate, dividing my time between reading and swallowing. The workers file out of the tavern. I stay a little longer. I don't have to punch a time card. Today I have to finish pruning and put the branches in a pile. Tomorrow I'll burn them.

The woman stands up, comes forward and approaches the spot where I'm sitting, fast and direct. I force my eyes to look straight at her nose, where her nostrils expel a little air after her words. "I have a new number. Use this one," and she leaves her name and a number on the tablecloth. I cover it with my hand, which is almost clean. I don't waste time washing up for my lunch break.

I see her standing. I get up to match her surprise gesture and say, "It's always a pleasure to see you." She puts her two hands around mine. "Say hi to your family." "Thank you, I'll tell them." The guy is at the door. She turns around and I sit back down.

What's gotten into me? "Thank you, I'll tell them." What am I, one of the living dead? Who am I going to tell? I haven't got anyone.

What does a fine woman like her want from a fifty-year-old gardener sitting in the corner of a tavern? Never met her before. She's young and I've come here after being in South America for twenty years. I'm here by accident. I found a job in a garden at a big house up the hill and I come down here at noon to relax and be around people. This is the first time she's come by.

I sink into thought. The owner comes by with a half carafe for us to split. "You're a gentleman," I tell him, "you have good house wine and a working man doesn't have to worry about getting heartburn on his afternoon shift."

"I used to work with my hands, too," he says.

"You even serve foreigners, and let Africans sit down at a table to eat and leave them alone."

"It doesn't cost me anything and my wife doesn't complain."

I nod my agreement.

"What's your story?" he asks. "I like a man who reads."

"It's how I keep myself company."

He looks me in the face, which is a good way to ask a question.

"I'm alone. I was in South America for many years and now I'm back. I don't know many people. I live in the old part of town."

To show that I have nothing more to say I lift my glass. "Thanks. To your health!" He's been seeing me here for a month. Sooner or later he deserves to know something about me. This seems to be good enough for him. He smiles, clinks his glass against mine and we drink.

He's the same age as me but wears it better.

The first time I came to his place I asked to taste his wine. He gave me a glass and threw in a plate of black olives. "If you don't like them you don't have to pay," he said.

I swish the wine around my mouth, ease it back into my throat. It is good. We make a deal. I come every day and he gives me whatever he's got, just a soup and some house wine.

"I have some sage in a vase that smells like fresh walnut, I'll bring it by tomorrow," I say.

"It's a long walk from the old part of town." Yes, I get up at five, but I don't mind. The smell of the sea comes in on the breeze.

The house creaks in the early morning. Stone, wood, yawning. The house quiets down when it smells the coffee. All it takes to fill a room is a pot of coffee on the stove.

I remember the card in my hand and slip it between the pages of the book. The owner stands up. It's time for me to go.

I have to dig a hole for an oak tree being delivered tomorrow. I work for a man who films documentaries. I know him from before I went to South America. He's the son of a Calabrian tailor who moved north to work in a factory, trading the precision of the needle for the slamming of the press against metal.

Craftsmen with good hands whose skills had been honed and then sold, shackled to four exhausting movements.

He leaves me in charge of the garden. He doesn't want a vegetable garden or livestock, even if there's enough land for everything. When he was a student and I was a worker, we used to be communists, a word hanging from the coatrack of the past century.

There's something I like about his face: so many others are embittered but his face still has an air of goodness and a nose as firm as a prow. His name is Mimmo. He enjoys talking about his father, who locked himself away in a factory to give his children a future.

Calabria is filled with the past: the olive trees planted by his grandparents, the house made from raw, rough-hewn stone. At the end of the day there's always something to put on the table, but there's no future.

Many of us from the old days are still around. We've all broken away from home. Not him. He still does his Sundays, his savings, the bits of advice that make up a family kitchen.

Even now I still see him as a quiet boy staring at the ground with his nose at a ninety-degree angle from the sidewalk while the other kids are talking dirty. I'm from the south, too, and I like people who say no without opening their mouths. They say their no's without making a big deal about it.

Twenty years later here he is, a filmmaker. Call him lucky. But some luck takes up with the first comer, dumb luck that leaves you high and dry and latches onto the next guy. But there's smart luck, too, that spots the right person and slowly tries him on.

And the living meet again. He remembers the nights in Turin, the tavern-keeper who puts on my tab the wine the kids used to drink, along with some olives and a few slices of salami. Nights you never want to go to sleep. The tavern-keeper who doesn't close till the last man gets up to leave.

The last men are still around, but not the tavern-keepers.

He remembers me punching out after the second shift, at around eleven o'clock at night. We'd meet up and talk about how the day went, whether there'd been any fights in the shop, or whether they'd gotten into any trouble at school or on the road.

A new move every day. Turin, a city of pawns rising up against the rest of the chessboard. The gates are never locked. The worker's brigade won't allow it. You can't tell the last from the first, the good-looking from the ugly, the young from the old, the gypsies from the well-heeled. He laughs at the memory. "Back then communism used to be poor kids who knew how to look good."

It happens then and never again.

It's also luck, not having a good job, a luck that comes from before, from living in an age that was less unfair to kids. To change the subject I ask, "So, what do you do?" He, king of the narrow face, laughs beneath his massive nose.

"It's been a while since I've heard you say hello," he says. "What do I do? I do a job where you have to hold together a bunch of people. Make one mistake and they send you packing."

"What's the problem?" I ask. "Where could you go wrong? Tell the story of the world, you'll never go wrong. As long as you love it."

Then he asks about me, but I don't dwell on my misadventures in Argentina, the unbridled wrongs, the search for life. He offers me a job and I gladly accept it.

Before saying good-bye I tell him a story. "I'm on a construction site and my helper is a man about my age, under fifty. He's a Kurd, a former writer, he speaks English. You meet interesting men on construction sites: castaways, drifters, sailors grounded for life. He has scars over one eye.

"'What happened?' By way of an answer the Kurd waves his hand toward his back. For us Italians that means water under the bridge. I'm not sure what it means in Kurdish.

"At lunch I ask him if he wants a coffee. He says no. I pour him some from my thermos anyway.

"One day he pulls out a sheet of paper with English writing. It says that the police in a country that shall remain nameless throw him in jail, giving him a daily ration of beatings. They ruin his eyes. One heals. The other doesn't.

"But a typo turns the word 'eyes' into 'yes.' His 'yes' is ruined by beatings. And the typo is right. All of his yesses are ruined. He hardly ever speaks a dented 'yes,' except in exchange for an offer of coffee or a hand in mixing lime.

"The beatings hurt his yesses more than his eyes. Some mistakes contain another truth."

I say this last part to bring the story to a close.

To keep it going he asks what I have in my pocket. A book, I say. Which one? A used book. I read books that are on their last legs. Why? I'll tell you another time. His hand goes toward my jacket pocket but not inside. It hangs there.

I read used books because fingerprint-smudged and dog-eared pages are heavier on the eye. Because every book can belong to many lives. Books should be kept in public places and step out with passersby who'll hold onto them for a spell. Books should die like people, consumed by aches and pains, infected, drowning off a bridge together with the suicides, poked into a potbellied stove, torn apart by children to make paper boats. They should die of anything, in other words, except boredom, as private property condemned to a life sentence on the shelf.

"I'll tell you another time," I tell him, on the verge of saying good-bye.

So I find myself spending my days in a garden tending trees and flowers and keeping to myself in more ways than one, lost in passing thoughts, songs, the pause of a cloud that lifts the sun and load from your back.

I walk through the field with a new apple tree to plant.

I set it down, turn it around, examine the nubs of new branches seeking their way in the surrounding space.

A tree needs two things: sustenance in the earth and beauty above it. They are concrete creatures driven by a force of elegance. The beauty they need is wind, light, birds, crickets, ants, and a starry threshold toward which the branches can point their patterns.

Beauty is the engine in the trees that drives their lymph upward. In nature only beauty contradicts gravity. Without beauty the tree can't manage. So I stop at one spot in the field and ask, "Is this where you want to be?"

I don't expect the tree to answer, to make a sign in the fist I have wrapped around its trunk, but I like having a word with the tree. It feels the edges, the horizons, and it's looking for an exact spot to rise. A tree hears comets, planets, masses and swarms. It hears the storms on the sun and the locusts on its back with the same vigilant attention. A tree is a union of the close and the perfect far.

If it comes from a nursery and has to take root in unknown soil, a tree is as confused as a country boy on his first day at the factory. So I take it for a walk before digging a hole for it.

At home I flatten out the page in front of my plate and take a second look at the piece of paper. Her name is Laila, two syllables from a nursery rhyme, an accent sitting atop the first vowel like a bolt of lightning: Làila.

The piece of paper is laying there.

I chew on a slice of cheese and read the book, but I'm distracted by the white patch laying crosswise over the vertical wood-grain of the table.

So I stand up, go out to the street to look for a telephone. I leave everything on the table, even the piece of paper. I realize this in the phone booth.

These setbacks amuse me. During the day the body obeys and obeys everything I ask of it, but once its share is done it balks, tells me to take a hike, sends me packing, chasing the wind, teases me silly. I think it's right. The body's a good beast of burden, and when it goes back indoors it wants to stay there.

I go up and down the road and I'm back with the number.

"Laila?"

"Yes?" I hear her voice, like a freshly opened bottle, cheerful and guttural.

"At my fingertips I have the number and name that you decided to give me."

"I want to see you again."

"I'm fifty and I'm a gardener."

"Alright. When?"

"Gardening I do every day, being fifty just recently."

She snorts, I hope it's a smile, and tells me that I've got good reflexes. She wants to see me again.

I don't think it's a good idea to keep her on the phone too long, so I say yes.

"Do you have a telephone?" she asks.

"No. I don't have a car, a record player or even a washing machine. But I do have a refrigerator."

"Let me take you out for dinner," she says.

"I'm too old to handle a waiter bringing the bill to a woman rather than to me."

"At my place, then?" I accept.

"Have you got a pen?"

"I wish!"

"So you'll have to memorize my address." She tells me the where and when.

"You keep giving me numbers and names. What are you, Laila, a code book?"

"Will you remember them?"

"If I don't, I'll call."

"So we're on," she says.

"Listen, Laila, you wouldn't happen to want my name?"

"Not right away," she replies.

"Well, it's not as pretty as yours," I say.

"You like it?"

"Like the beginning of a song. You learn the music in an instant and the words come later."

I hang up. At home I eat, read. No more pieces of paper laying crossways between me and my nighttime habits.

What is Laila like. I try to imagine. She's someone who looks men up and down, a general who from a thousand-soldier formation can pick out the men to raise through the ranks.

They look at her in the streets, but she looks first.

I make things up. Laila weighs you on the scale of her quick eyes and finds you lacking.

What does she see in me? A cardboard face from working outdoors.

Maybe she likes the kind of guy at a tavern who turns pages rather than rolling bread crumbs into balls.

She's tall, doesn't wear any trinkets around her fingers or neck.

She speaks with a dark, throaty voice. She has capable hands.

High cheekbones to summon a smile, a nice geometric face, full mouth, healthy bite. It must be nice to watch her eat.

Soft temples hinted at by a lock of hair. Strong nostrils for drawing in air.

I want to bring her a vase of sage from my garden, so I can tell her where it comes from.

I think of the things I won't tell her, the layers of life to peel away.

I'll tell her about the sage on Pag Island, a goat pasture that produces the best-smelling cheese in the Mediterranean.

I'll tell her about Christmas struffoli, made by a grandmother who late at night rolls thousands of little dough balls to fry and then coat with honey.

About life in the saltworks, the red algae in the purification ponds where the salt forms into crystals and blinds the onlooker. The salt-worker never gazes below the horizon. He stares at the sky, which is less glaring than the ground even at noontime.

At sunset red is everywhere you look. Even the shade is a smattering of rust.

And I'll stop there. No sense flaunting past history.

It's dawn on the train taking me into the city. At one point the darkness gives way and fades. A little light to read by. The car is old, it rattles and shakes.

I look at the land, think of my garden. Growing trees gives me satisfaction.

A tree is like a population rather than a person. It struggles to plant itself, it takes root in secret. If it survives, the generations of leaves begin.

Then it is welcomed by the surrounding land and pushed upward.

The earth yearns for tallness, the heavens. It crashes continents into each other to create ridges.

It rummages through the roots so it can expand in the air with the wood.

And if the land turns into a desert, it makes dust so it can escape. Dust is a veil, it migrates, crosses seas. The scirocco wind carries it from Africa, steals spices from markets and seasons the rain.

The world is a master builder!

So go the lurching thoughts of a railroad passenger. With my gardener's calculations, prunings, seedings, forecasts of blossoming and fruit, I'm like the egg teaching the chicken. Down comes a spit of hail, a pane of frost and consider yourself served, lord of the gardens.

This is how I see it: the hard work is nothing, just a way to make a living. But what matters is living with your head between your feet, your face down to tend the goings-on below. What matters is keeping your neck craned over the ground, caring more about it than about people.

In the time remaining this makes it nice to get involved with other people, to understand each other at a glance, shave for a date with woman, throw yourself bodily against oppression.

I've spent more of my life looking at the ground, water, clouds, walls, and tools than at faces. And I like them.

Now I let my mind wander over Laila's face: cheekbones as shiny as copper, pouting lips, mismatched pieces. Now that I think about it, I can't remember her whole face.

I'm the last one to get off the train, the grim habit of a man used to making sure he isn't being followed. After the arrivals swarm away, the end of the platform is empty and you have to be careful. Habits from another lifetime have stayed with me.

In the garden I slip on overalls over my clothes. Jack Frost is in the air to keep the ground hard and make it crunch beneath my shoes.

Below the trunk of the laurel is the pale orange of a robin separated from its branch, fallen from the cold like an open leaf.

The roughness of the North blows in my face. Better to shave not in the morning but at night. I have my razor with me. After work I'm going to Laila's house. In the toolshed I pack what I need to sleep since there are no more trains after supper.

I loosen the ground below the laurel trees. Their thick evergreen leaves protect the sparrows. At night the birds fight for the warmest spot, close to the trunk. They fight to stay alive. Then they release a sigh of appeasement. I think they're praying.

I only prune the laurels in spring, when they're not acting as shelters for the sparrows. I like burning the remains of their branches. They give off a smoke that confounds the senses and reminds you of the deceased. In the midst of that smoke I sit down at noon with my black olives.

On days like this I can see the geometry clearly. The living are not at a ninety-degree angle above the dead. Instead they're parallel. The sickle is not curved like the moon but like an egg. Bread rises, copying the shape of the baker's palm. Bringing it to your mouth is like shaking his hand.

If you keep quiet while your body is working, thoughts of swimming and flying come and go at will. From a long-ago April I can see the sky of Jericho, white with storks migrating from Africa to the rooftops of Europe.

In front of the tavern-keeper's soup I finish a story describing the city of Odessa.

Never seen the Black Sea. How can I claim to know the Mediterranean if I don't know the boundless rivers from the depths of Russia that keep its waters even?

I can hardly keep track of the things I don't know, but every now and then comes an ignorance that makes me nostalgic.

I browse through pages about a city of figs, bandits, sailors, and Jews.

Meanwhile the tavern is filling up with dark men chilled to the bone. I invite three of them to take the empty seats at my table, order a liter of wine to share, and apologize for going back to my book.

They belong to three different ages and peoples. They eat something plucked from their pockets. Our hands fill the table.

I read about Odessa and listen to the ebb and flow of their breathing.

The cold outside compresses the lungs, which spread to warm the blood once they've taken shelter.

The men accept a cup of coffee, then leave together after shaking hands.

That afternoon the holm oak arrives. I arrange the roots in the hole, stake it between three posts, fertilize and water. It's already a nice little tree, but it's going to take a lot of effort and danger before it establishes itself as a grown-up. Sometimes trees get sad and lose their will to live. I sing as a way of welcoming it. I wrap it to give it strength.

Soon it's dark. I wash my face, pass the razor over it. I don't use soap. All I have to do is leave the water on for a minute to moisten the skin and it comes away smooth.

I rub my hands together roughly to remove the shadow of the earth. Then I wrap an old tie around my neck and go.

I come in, give her hand a squeeze and turn around to hang up my coat. While I'm standing with my back to her I feel her finger pass over my neck from one ear to the other. I don't understand the gesture and turn around slowly. She says I have two parallel wrinkles like her father, two cuts, she says.

I ask whether I look like him from the front, too, but no, she has another thought. She takes my hands, turns them around, says that my palms look like his but not the back of my hands. In other words a wrong side resembles, a right side does not.

She has on a tight dress that touches her body in all the right places and a sweater as white as an almond blossom. In the meantime we're both still standing at the front door.

She takes me into a big room. I see a kitchen, table that's been set, chairs, sofa, big paintings. I stop noticing.

I hardly know myself. Without embarrassment I sit down and arrange my pants neatly over my knee and ask where she's from. Russia and Scotland on her mother's side, Sicily and Liguria on her father's.

"You're a princess, you've got geography in your blood."

Her name comes from a Russian grandmother born on the right bank of the Neva. "Nébo na Névoi," the Sky Over Neva, is a song, a single strophe left behind on the borders of her childish sleep, where nursery rhymes grow and a grandmother's voice crackles in dreams.

She asks whether I too am a prince by mixed blood.

"No, my parents are from the same place and so are my grandparents."

But I invent a hodgepodge of ancestors. "At night I feel a Greek nostalgia for the stars piled high in glossaries, for the calculations of the planets, for the rule of the comets."

Laila sits on the armrest, so I look at her from below and like it.

I continue. "In the open night I realize that science was moved by beauty, by the desire to understand it."

Faced by a woman, the Neapolitan in me comes out, the wish to make her laugh.

If you don't laugh first, kisses are insipid. This is something I don't tell her.

At work I belong to a sea of sudden squalls, unlike the known, forewarned storms of the Atlantic. This is why I take in stride whatever weather may come.

In the mirror I feel a Jewish shudder when I shave below my temples, a French nose before cheese, and with wine in my glass I feel in my palm the tickling of an ancestor tilling the over-grazed terraces of the Piedmont hills.

Laila moves her quick eyes to my face. She's surveying me. I give her time and continue. Before the sea I feel the prudence of an island peasant who goes down to the marina in winter, when the land has to be abandoned, to try his luck at fishing.

"Do you really know yourself so well or are you making it up?" she asks.

"Some things I concoct, some I glean from my senses, some I thirst for."

She excuses herself, stands up, and seems much taller—or is it me that's sunken into the sofa while she's been on the armrest?

"Wine?" Yes.

"Cheese?" Yes.

I get up, too, take a tinfoil package from my pocket, and open my sage leaves on the table. I tear one into little pieces over a slice.

"It has such a strong smell," she says.

"It's an incense that'll send the devils scurrying," I say.

She sits close, asks me to mince a leaf over a second slice.

"It takes two hands to make sage into incense," she says, sniffs, the profile of her nose forming a narrow angle with the plane of the table.

This is how I see angles: if they're acute they're good, if they're obtuse they're bad and if they're ninety degrees they're even.

She makes as if to clink our glasses in a toast. I turn my hand to rub my knuckles against hers. "First you toast with the fingers, then with the glass." Where did I learn that? In another world, in a time when it was strange to live and find yourself awake the next day, still alive.

"You'll tell me about it later," she says.

I shake my head in a minimal no. She doesn't notice the no.

"You seem like someone who knows a lot," she says.

I disagree. "I don't even know which side the bread is buttered on."

She laughs.

There's a smile, I think, and I realize how her mouth widens at the sides and her tongue sparkles between her teeth and my nose is itching to lean into her laughter.

She asks what kind of work I do. "I'm a blue-collar gardener. I'm often on my knees. I wear out the knees of my pants and sew them up like new."

"How's the soil?" she asks, and expects a joking answer that's low, too low.

But I don't. I act serious and say something else. "There are two kinds of soil," I say and turn toward where she is seated next to me. "One kind has water underneath. You make a hole and it comes up. It's easy land."

"The other depends on the sky, its only source. It's lean, thievish, can steal water from the wind and the night, and as soon as it has a little, it spends it all on colors kept in the marrow of stones, gives energy to the sugars in fruits and brazenly sprinkles aromas everywhere. That's the kind of soil sage comes from."

She listens to me, her lips tight, asks if I write these things down.

"No, I write nothing, I read, and happily."

"What about letters? You know, love letters?"

Her question brings to mind a story rather than an answer. I want to tell it to her, but I'm also hungry, I say.

And we sit down to the plates and she ladles out a good soup of lentils and fava beans. I swallow two spoonfuls, then I speak.

"A woman comes to see me some time ago.

"I open the door, she's intact, straight out of twenty years' past, a distance she wears as if it were no more than a streetcar ride.

"She wants to hear some news about me, wants to see if two pieces of time match up. She pulls out my letters. I read through them for the first time. You know, when I write them I don't reread them. I close and mail them, then as now.

"Beneath the weathered cardboard of my face, I feel the face I used to have, before changing the world, when it still felt like all-purpose dough. I tell her that what she has to do is bring to the boy from the old days the embrace she conceals inside. That she is still whole and can find someone like him again. What I tell her, in other words, is: I'm not me."

"'If you're not you,' she says, 'you never were you.'"

"She stands up from the table, puts her coat on, and walks out, calm, splendid, speechless. Today I still don't know if she's right."

I tell this story and Laila asks why.

"I see old poets receiving prizes for verses written in their youth. None of them says, 'It's not me.' I can't act like them. I have to say, 'The award you bring by visiting, perpetual teenager of twenty years ago, is being accepted by my uncle. I am the decrepit uncle of the guy that wrote those letters.'

"The only thing I manage to say is, 'It's not me,' and I drink the wine left in the woman's glass."

I place my hand over the glass in front of me, which is better than the hand from that earlier time.

"And the letters?" she asks.

"She left them there."

"Do you still have them?"

I smile. "No."

With her knuckles, Laila caresses the back of my hand. I don't feel like making a return gesture. I stay quiet.

"I like the way you're made," she says, "like a river stone."

I look at some points of her face. I feel an impulse to stand up, push the table away, reach her side.

"You like me," she says. It's not a question.

How do you answer?

"So do you," she says.

"Of course I do, not even when I was twenty do I remember being close to such beauty." But my words are just a reflex.

"You're lying, but it sounds nice anyway," she says.

And she stands up and turns on some music and makes me stand. We're the same height.

"I remember the dances at the village festivals," I say. "I miss the parties that are good for tapping your feet around a girl."

I place my arm around her gently. I still feel the shape of her ribs. In my left hand her hand feels like fresh bread, I bring it close to my nose.

I rock back and forth like an autumn branch, I shed leaves. Up close, her face sighs. Rather than confuse, it sweeps away thought.

"What are you thinking of?" she asks.

I look at her hair, recognize the flick of the wrist that arranges it in waves, think that the wood of her hairbrush is like the Atlantic wind plowing long waves.

Our foreheads feel as if they're getting closer, I hear her describing me now. She says that I'm stubborn and that's how people give freedom to others. They have no followers so they persist without turning back.

I keep drifting slowly in the music, her soft breathy voice stirs my blood. Not her beauty, not the occasion: her words. And my nose widens when our bodies touch in the middle.

"Are you sniffing?" she asks.

"Yes, I am sniffing your words."

"Are you stubborn or not?"

Much, much less. "Whatever you may think of me, trim it a little, take it down a peg, and I'll answer here I am."

"Here I am," says Laila.

Her forehead advances, a simmering slowness, leans against mine, a lock of her hair over my short-haired temples and her breath rising into my nostrils and my breathing so I can't even hear and we're so near we have to stand still.

With her hand she pushes the nape of my neck so our faces are crushed into the place where our mouths meet.

Now only our noses are breathing.

Then it's the hands' turn to move beyond their restlessness.

We say nothing, embarrassed to be holding each other.

I go slowly to keep from hurtling my force against her, to allow her force to grow, too.

She's on top of me, dealing low blows to my chest. That's how you cut down trees, one blow to cleave and a twist to free the steel for the impact. Laila taps away at my chest. I proudly resist for a long time, like a tree clamping down on the acidic iron cutting into it. I fall down and so does she.

I notice her caresses drying me off. I sleep for a few breaths.

Then I look for my clothes. I live far away.

"Stay," she says.

"If you want company, fine. Otherwise I'd rather not get in the way."

"I want you to get in the way of my sheets," she says. Then she asks if I want to talk a little.

A little. I ask how it is that she's alone.

"My job."

"Do you make a living from solitude?"

"No, from men, I go out with men for money. Not on the streets, on dates."

I say nothing. It's not as if she's handing me the bill. She asks if I'm repelled by her. "No."

"Now you know."

"No," I say. "Now I know your intention to tell me. This is the really wonderful news. Nothing I say could ever equal this, Laila."

"You wouldn't want to," she says.

"That's true, too," I say.

"It doesn't matter. As long as I don't repel you."

We remain stretched out in half an embrace. She says "Hold me" and I take her with my other arm, too, and lay it on top of her. And I squeeze her a little. "Is this all right for a 'hold me'?" She laughs at herself right behind my ear.

"That'll make me fall in love with you," I say. It's a lie but I say it anyway.

"Men never fall in love with a working girl," she says.

Maybe her customers don't, I say, but a ne'er-do-well gardener like me just might.

We're laying down, she looks at my nose, I stare at the ceiling.

I remember nights without even a leaf between my skull and the sky.

I remember days and moves that passed by like a crack, betting on bad luck to somehow endure.

"A fugitive doesn't run toward open space but into many barred paths. I drive myself mad with U-turns, detours. At night I seek the open air, I travel by foot, I head south. The world is on my shoulders. Even the stars are dogs at my heels. Now, here with you, I'm waiting for sleep and thinking of the southern sky."

"Which south?" she asks.

"The south of the world," I say. "Sagittarius, Lupus, Centaur, Vela, Southern Cross."

Do I know the stars? "We're on a first-name basis, on intimate terms, but I don't really know them. We've only been introduced from afar."

She laughs. "What were you doing down there?"

"War."

"Which one?"

"Just one, there's always one somewhere."

"Soldiers are a good match for working girls," she says.

"I wouldn't know," I say.

"Your face does," she says, and touches me with the back of her finger and lets it glide down my face. "Faces are writings."

"Hands are too," I say, "and clouds, tiger pelts, peapods, and the leaping of tuna on the water's surface are writings. We learn alphabets and don't know how to read trees. Oaks are novels, pines are grammar books, grapevines psalms, ramblers proverbs, firs the closing remarks of a defense lawyer. Cypresses are accusations, rosemary a song, laurel a prophecy."

"All I have to do is read your face," she says.

"Which page do you prefer?"

"The last, the nape of the neck with my father's parallel wrinkles. There are men," she says, "who tell their secrets after they drink. But you're one of those who only lets something slip on the threshold of sleep."

Her voice becomes rough, sandpaper rubbing against wood. I feel sleepy but I start talking and realize that I'm falling behind my words, I'm helpless to stop them. I hear myself saying, "There's something in me that you find in many men of the world: loves, gunshots, thorny sentences and no desire to talk. Dozens of us are like that. Living is what matters, looking at the palm of your hand at night and knowing that tomorrow it will be fresh again, that the seamstress of the night stitches skin, mends scabs, patches rips, and relines exhaustion."

I hear my words coming to my voice on their own.

Now she apologizes. Her voice is clear again, like water on my face. She hugs me, repeats that she's sorry, I don't know what for, I don't ask, I hold her against my chest until I fall asleep.

I LEAVE WITH THE darkness. In the garden I work quickly to keep warm. I put in a stone walkway next to the grapevine rows.

A tall man, African, older, calls to me from the gate. I go to him, he introduces himself, shakes my hand. He asks how I'm doing, how the work is going. I reply, out of the good habit of making small talk before getting to the main subject.

I don't know what he has to tell me. In the meantime I let him in and invite him to the toolshed for a coffee that I prepare on a camp burner.

He gladly accepts. He has good teeth for a smile. Here he's a day laborer, at home he raised livestock. He comes to Italy often, never for more than a year, then he goes back home. In his mouth he's sucking on something. It's not a candy, it's an olive pit. He loves dark olives, the force of the oil embedded in a wood that's hard to chew.

He likes the taste of bone and turns the pit around in his mouth until it's smooth and the flavor is gone.

"Olives keep me company," he says.

A handful lasts him all day.

The coffee climbs, gurgles fragrantly in the coffeepot's throat. Before drinking it he says a prayer of thanks. "You don't pray?" he asks.

"I don't."

"I pray," he says, "before everything that I bring to my mouth. I pray to connect the day to its support, like a pole and a tomato plant. I bless this coffee of friendship."

"Maybe for someone from Africa it's easier to tie the earth to the sky with string."

He holds the white cup in his stone-gray palm.

We drink sitting next to each other on the bench. I tell him that his Italian is good. He replies that he likes the language better than the rest.

"Hard life here?" I ask.

"No. It's good. People give you no satisfaction, but life is good. You go out, feel like chewing the fat," he says, "and nothing—here people don't answer you. They give you no satisfaction," he repeats, "but life is good."

I put the cups away, ask if I can help him with anything. "Yes," he says, and points to the mimosas. They're in their first bloom. He asks if he can't have a bunch to sell in bouquets.

I cut a good armful. He's happy, asks how much. "Nothing, there's plenty and it's good for the plant to lose weight. Come again while they're still in bloom." He wants to pay, to owe me nothing.

"So treat me to a bottle of wine when the blossoms are gone, we'll drink it together."

He sits down on the ground, pulls out a strong knife and starts making the bouquets. Then he leaves, black filled with yellow. Each color shines in the other's arms.

The blankets left in the shed remind me of Laila's bed. My empty stomach makes me think of her embrace.

On the road to the tavern I try to remember. Only the pieces come to me. The last thing I remember is her elbow, surrounded by peach fuzz.

I set the soup between myself and the book leaning against the carafe.

It's sunny outside and the room is no longer filled with the ice-cold South of yesterday. I eat.

The spoon is a reader's friend, scooping from the plate almost by itself. The fork requires more attention.

I savor a potato soup peppered with red spice while reading a port adventure seasoned with written smells. I don't realize that Laila is standing there, waiting for me to look up.

I see her when I turn the page—damn—I jump to

my feet, take my glasses off, hold out my hand, move the chair, try to show a little attentiveness to make up for her waiting.

I don't give out my phone number or address so she has to guess. "Wait for a phone call from me after work?"

"Liar," she says, sneaks a peek at the book's title, orders fish.

I look at her, I say: "You're amazing, Laila, you plant your elbows on the table like a queen who clears a space wherever she rests her weight. You keep your back as straight as the bow of a boat on the water. What are you doing at a table with a gardener?"

"Fishing for a compliment," she says, then she gets irritated by someone staring at her, so I turn around out of curiosity and a man turns his face the other way. She says, "It's comfortable being with a man, like a gardener, for example."

I put the book to one side of the table and think that now it looks like an "equal" sign.

She and I are facing each other like two numbers with that mathematical symbol to the side. I don't know what kind of operation we are.

"What am I thinking?" I tell her about the black man with the mimosas. She says to save her a branch. She places my palm over her hand. I'm a little embarrassed. She isn't. She's the queen of men.

Long fingers, spacious hand that resembles her mouth, a willful wrist. She keeps her hand over mine, says that it's like holding a stone. She says that she feels like throwing it against a window and running.

I'm not embarrassed. For five minutes I've been in love with a woman who goes with men, I love her with an *olé* in my eyes.

It won't last. Why should it? It'll stop where it wants. In the meantime I'll love her: me, a little daft from surrounding myself with books, nails that are never even, short gray hair that's almost all in place, wide feet, good teeth, a back thickened like carved wood. I love a woman who has happened to me, a couple of feet straight ahead.

I become absorbed in a kind of geometry: I unite the two points of her eyes, sketch a line that goes up to a painting of mountains and down to a sleeping cat. "Your eyes combine the sleep of the cat and a forest of larches."

"I don't understand," she says.

I explain it to her; she pretends to be upset: "Do you have any other manias?"

"Yes, no matter where I am, even indoors, I need to know where the cardinal points are. The front door," and I lower my voice as if I were telling a secret, "is to the north."

She acts as if she's in on it.

"You're to the south and I feel like someone who is going back down there."

I take her to the garden, cut off a branch, now she, too, wears the little yellow pompoms. She asks if I am going to her house afterward.

"Yes."

I get back to work.

I'm a little tired. The sun is leaning into the earth, so heavily I don't need to put any energy into the tools to warm up.

I admit that my tiredness comes from the exhausting night and dispel the thought of postponing another visit to Laila's. I'm sick of saving up.

I loosen the soil around the plants with a hoe, to tuck a little air under the upturned grass.

I remember the days in the south filled with trouble, ruined by death that tears away clumps of us folks, stuffs thousands of the living, freshly plucked, into its sack. Days when love is an exchange of deep hugs, a need for bonding. And behind every finished embrace, behind every giving each other peace, a tough good-bye remains unsaid.

Strange to know you're lost every day and yet never say farewell to each other.

Today an exchange of farewells would be enough for me. To forget.

I loosen the soil and feel like I'm loosening up names. Here inside Europe, at the antipode of Argentina, time doesn't dig in its heels like a horse, an applause, a blast of wind. It fans out slowly like a drizzle.

There is nothing of mine to protect here.

I obey your comic urgency, Laila, I think to myself on my way home, surrounded by men on the evening train, disheartened from exhaustion.

We are layered with clothing, eggs packed in crates.

At home under the shower I admit that I'm too hairy to be an egg.

Love returns, so I remember my first love while taking the train.

At twenty I make a few tries at a mediocre love. With one girl I have an urge to go to the movies together, with another to go for a walk in a different city. I look for them, they avoid me, I write them a few letters.

They don't work out but they don't stir love.

I forget about them by learning how to climb mountains.

Then I meet Dvora one summer.

There are creatures assigned to each other that never manage to meet and end up adjusting to another person's love in order to heal the absence. They are wise.

At twenty I have no knowledge of embraces and I decide to wait. I wait for the creature assigned to me. I'm vigilant, I learn to scan the faces in a crowd in a few seconds. There are methods for teaching you how to speed-read a book. I learn how to speed-read a crowd. I sift through it, discard everything, not even a grain of those faces remains on my retina. I always know she isn't there, she, the one assigned to me.

I don't have in mind a picture that's supposed to match a face. The assignment doesn't depend on the eyes, although I don't know what it does depend on. I have to wait till I meet her to find out what she looks like.

To wait. This is my verb when I'm twenty, a dry infinitive that doesn't ooze with anxiety, that doesn't drool with hope. I wait in vain.

I meet Dvora in the mountains. I'm on the wall of the Tofana di Rozes pillar in the Dolomites. It's noon and my two-man rope is in the area of the roofs.

Dvora's climbing a *via ferrata* opposite the pillar. She pops out from behind and at one point finds herself facing the wall where two guys right in the center are tied to a one-inch-thick rope, which from a distance must look like a clothesline.

My face is up against the rock and I'm scaling the second roof. When I plant my foot on it Dvora lets out a cry of victory, brighter than noontime: "*Olè!*" Her voice catches me from behind and I recognize it, it's her, the one assigned to me, I know it right away and I feel like I already know that the sign I am awaiting is not a face but a voice.

I look upward and see only sky and downward I see only the void. From the opposite peak she repeats the trill of her *olè* and raises an arm and I twist my neck and see a tiny point of life standing straight above an abyss of crumbled rock.

I take the bandana from around my neck and wave it while I'm still on the rope and don't care whether the other arm has to suffer the pain of working for two and not waving. And I throw the red bandana into the air and it glides and plummets like a wounded wing. And I call out "*olè*" and my rope partner shouts to hurry up to make it to a berth, but for a minute the only thing I can do and say is "*olè*," then I shout the name of the hut where you descend to after climbing the mountain. And I don't see her anymore.

We touch the peak in two hours, after speeding up our climb. We throw ourselves into the descent like greased lightning and instead it's still early afternoon and full sun. And we make it to the hut and she's not there. My partner goes back down. I stay seated, my back to the door, waiting to hear her voice.

And she arrives. Here comes Dvora. I feel bees in my blood, a bear in my heart. Every heartbeat is a paw that crushes the beehive.

She gives me her hand, I know that I'll never let go.

Dvora, Argentinian, is touring Europe as a graduation prize.

Dvora, light in her old, sun-baked hiking boots, her hands chapped from the *ferrata* cable, her eyebrows bleached by the salt of her sweat. Her smile is aimed at my hair, ruffled by a secret wind even indoors.

I'm coming with you, Dvora.

She says, "We're climbing the Tofana di Rozes."

"Yes, tomorrow morning, by the *ferrata* that passes through the big explosion room in the Castelletto mine. From the first world war, when soldiers were dispatched to tear away inches of rock through gigantic efforts. Hundreds of yards in a hole that spirals upward. For stretches you need a flashlight on your head like a miner."

I make the shape of a headlamp with my hands. "Like Moses," she says, laughs, says "*olè.*"

We sleep at the hut, stretch out, each in our own sleeping bags, close together. We hold hands and fall asleep in an instant.

The next day we enter the dark silence of a grotto carved in a ceiling.

I tell Dvora about the excavating machines that suck in air and spit out dust.

I tell of the boys sent up here to stumble between crevices and bullets, to hit the ground when a bomb shifts the air, who lived to surrender their eyes to the crows.

Dvora listens, breathes, climbs behind me tied to the other end of a rope. From a few holes chiseled to release the explosion, we measure the altitude we've reached and calm our breath.

We come out of the tunnel onto the shaded steps of the western wall and climb back up the intervals with an elastic spring in our legs. The neck seeks the heights after so many yards face down.

We cross rock terraces, passing through the remains of trenches where young men dreamt of growing old with a century that was still new. The way I am now dreaming of growing old with Dvora. War is when young men dream of becoming grandfathers.

There are stones blackened by campfires. We are walking in the footsteps of a younger generation transformed into wood and barbed wire.

We climb the Tofana along the side. Beneath us lies

the Travenanzes Valley, illuminated by the white of its stream.

Dvora asks me the names, repeats them with relish, as if she were tasting the first fruit.

The last stretch of the *ferrata* is a rigged cable that takes you to the base of the final pyramid.

At the summit of the Tofana, Dvora kisses me and calls me *novio*, boyfriend, and I'm happier than a March hare. She calls me *basherte*, which in one of her six languages means "person destined for someone." And I like lovers' names and call her *novia* and *basherte*, too.

We sleep in our sleeping bags, each to his own, but keeping our heads close together. At night we knock heads and are wakened by the "Ouch!" and the laughter that follows.

Married love between us begins in Argentina.

I'm at Laila's door again with a bottle under my arm and a thought I blurt out at the entrance. I tell her immediately that it's the end of February and the apricot tree is already starting to bloom. The cold will dry its sap and it won't give fruit.

As a joke she asks whether the garden's owner will mind having no apricots. "No," I say, "but I can't stand my powerlessness to restrain the tree. I'm a gardener and I don't know how to keep it from rushing into bloom when it's still winter. And then I feel responsible for the garden."

"You'd think you were Adam," she says and closes the door.

I give her the bottle, she returns it with a corkscrew, goes to the stove to stir the sauce. A narrow back, backbone curved like a whip, arms and shoulders sprouting from the trunk. "What a beautiful tree you are," I say, holding her between me and the burner.

"You see branches everywhere," she says, but doesn't shake me off. "Are you falling in love, gardener?"

"No, I'm just going crazy."

"What's it like?"

"Nice."

The sauce and a handful of oregano already summon the summer. I hold a pinch and sniff it to notify my senses. Laila lands a cheerful kiss on my lips, with a quick smack. She's wearing an almond essence on her clothes.

With my nails I mince a tiny red spice, sprinkle it over the plate and ask whether she minds our age difference.

"On the contrary, we're not far enough apart," she says. "You bring out the child in me, when I used to hug grown-ups for the joy of squeezing. What about you?"

"I see the pain of miserly love in young people," I say. "You don't have that kind of melancholy on your face. But

I'm careful not to step on your feet when I speak with you. It's not like dancing. It's like a stone walkway with a little grass growing between the cracks. It's strong but I still try to tread carefully and not ruin it. At Muslim homes you leave your shoes outside. This is how I behave with you."

We eat slowly, in silence.

Facing a plate of food, my gestures slow down. Laila keeps time and I see her adagio become intense with grace. The desire to touch her grows dense.

Then I hear her voice breaking up, like the sounds on the threshold of sleep. I hear her asking me something and a part of me answering. Another part of me, where I am, listens to my voice go off on its own.

I start with music then sentences come to me from a distance and I don't know how to do anything to stop them.

They're killing all of us, we members of the rebellion.

We race from one hiding place to another.

We're wearing the stench of fear on our backs. The dogs can smell it on the street and chase after us.

In escape we seek our revenge.

Argentina tears a whole generation from the world like a madwoman pulling at her hair. It kills its children, wants to be done with them. We're the last.

I've been here for years in order to love a woman and now I'm caught up in a war.

At one roadblock shots ring out. They stop us. We're armed. There are two of us. My partner wounds a policeman and immediately gunfire goes through his throat and he dies at my feet.

His face is torn open by a bullet. His face gives me energy. I smell the release of his bowels and the stench drives me out.

From behind the car I come out into the open, take aim at the policemen's barrier. Their guns jam. I'm on top of them, shooting at a body that falls over the other one, who's wounded. I see the stunned face of a boy, not an enemy. I don't shoot at him, I flee.

So go the days, in rushes.

Money's grabbed from a bank to keep running.

Before I stop, I shoot a colonel, a single shot in a crowd on a Sunday sidewalk. Today I still don't know if he's alive or dead. Then I go south, where the land narrows, where it's stupid to flee.

They look for the last of us elsewhere.

I'm at a sailors' tavern and learn to move in the perpetual chaos of the lower Atlantic wind. It covers, hides, deafens, and doesn't come to speak.

I'm in no hurry. I wear the clothes of a sailor who waits for a berth and drinks.

The tavern-keeper has an Italian name, grandparents from Otranto, another kind of land's end surrounded by water. He asks when I'm going. There's a whaling ship on its way to the Malvinas Islands.

I'm at the bottom of the sack of my life. Any day I could be shaken out of it.

The tavern-keeper wants me to go. Maybe he's helping me. He arranges a berth for me as a mate on an Irish steamer.

Before climbing aboard I get rid of my guns.

For the first time in years my clothes feel light, my hands absentminded. The wind blows so hard it could take me in its arms. Without weapons, I weigh nothing.

I climb up the ladder, thinking of no one. I'm the last leaf on a tree. I break away without a push.

I don't think of the girl that I loved, that I followed till I became part of her country.

Now I know that she's at the bottom of the ocean, thrown into the open sea with her hands tied from a helicopter. She lived for me, died to give her eyes to the fish.

I climb aboard and for two days before departing I have a brush, paint, and wire brush to scrape away the briny rust.

I learn the ten men's names and their preference for onion. One guy eats them by the bite, like apples.

At the harbor's outlet the wind is sheer force, shattering waves and drenching beards.

I sleep in a hammock hanging from the beams in the hold, rocking over the engine room.

I'm forty and sleep so heavily you have to kick me to make me stop.

They call me the dead man. No one can sleep where I can.

No one knows how many lives it's been since I slept.

The voyage is a tenacious storm, the engine on low just to correct the drift.

The fishing is no good, twice as hard. It's a struggle for the net to snatch the fish from the waves. It tears, depriving sailors of their sleep.

After the wind, the beer tastes sweet.

On Sundays they pray, they're Catholics. The captain has shrapnel wounds in his face. One of the guys must have fought back before setting out to sea.

They take me with them because I reek of war, too.

I pay for my passage by working, but they don't need me.

The unspoken agreement is that they're leaving me on the islands. The only book is the Bible. I read it in bad light, in an iron shell, in the open sea.

I grow fond of David, who lays a single stone before Goliath and a single book, the Psalms, in the mouth of the world.

"I don't believe the writers but I believe their stories."

That's my answer to a freckle-faced sailor who asks if I have faith in God.

We work the fish, freeze it, and are at sea a month and a half.

When I disembark on Soledad Island in the Malvinas I can't walk. Without the sea below me I wobble and miss the wind that would fill my ears until I forgot. I am on English soil.

I stop at a tavern, the woman is a whaler's widow, Maria, Maria del Sol is her name.

I'm her cook. I tend her garden and keep watch over her wooly sheep.

At night we make noise. Maria's as strong as a sloop sailing against the sea. I'm standing up and pushing on the oars.

The fishermen laugh and drink a cloudy beer with me at night. Maria insults them but plays along with their jokes. I switch from fish to cheese.

The island is humid, with bogs where coal and plants waste away.

No trees, though. The wind mows them down like a gardener. There's some short grass and scabs of lichen and moss on the mounds. Scratched earth.

The sheep's lips are strong enough to tear away the short, tough skin of the pastures.

The fishing birds find a point where they hover, motionless, then break away from the sky's stillness and jab at a wave.

I wait. I have nothing to ask of time.

There are more animals than men, more women than men, everything is more numerous than men.

And years go by. I work, satisfy Maria, don't touch a dime, don't think.

On the radio I hear an Argentinian song again. The invasion is the next day.

Laila's voice interrupts me, ringing in both parts of my head.

I realize I've said a lot, so I drink a glass to slake my thirst and still my tongue.

"It was me," she says, "I made you speak."

"You're good at it," I say.

"Yes," she says in a voice, a second voice that comes loose.

"What do you think of my stories?" I ask.

"I love them," she says. "It's my job to make men talk, to tease information from their heads. With you I listen freely, I listen and learn to love the life that is written on your face."

"You've got men in the palm of your hand," I say.

"Yours is the hand I love," she replies.

"I won't slap you in the head because I'm nuts about you," she laughs.

"Don't extract any more stories from me. If I can't hold onto them, I'd rather tell you when I'm awake."

"Tomorrow I have to go," she says.

"Tomorrow," I say, "what do I know? Here we've got all the today we need." I stand up, pick her up in my arms and lay her down.

"Hold me, gardener, hold me. It's everything I need. Hold me. And don't ask questions."

"I wouldn't know what to ask."

"Do like you did with Maria," she says.

"And you do like Laila does."

Now nothing is strong enough to tear us apart.

THEN COME THE DAYS without.

Selim comes to the garden for the mimosas. He also wants to talk a little about his country, where they go barefoot so they can talk more freely.

"With your shoes on you can't speak, that's what we think." Without the naked sole of the foot on the ground, we are isolated, according to his language, that judging from its ringing sound must have a silver fishbone inside.

"It's the truth," I say, "the pure amen." Our whole history is a shoe separating us from the ground of the world. Shoe is home, car, book. Thinking about it like this makes me smile.

"What are you daydreaming about, gardener?"

I ask him where he lives, with a thought of putting him up. He replies that he stays at an abandoned house, without windows or doors, which he likes.

He says, "Over here you build with water from the earth. You get water from a well, from a fountain, from a river. In my country we build with water from the sky. We collect it and when we have a little, we make our mixture. Our houses are made from rain. They're more like clouds than houses."

And Selim laughs, he laughs at the houses of the world.

I feel separated from Laila, not from the earth, which I'm always on top of, always digging into with my hands.

Selim wants to pay, he's earned something.

"Forget about it. Without you the blossoms would still be here, inside a closed garden. You, instead, do the wind's work. You scatter them far, pin them to women's breasts. It would be exploitation if I took a percentage from the wind. Pay for drinks one night when there's no more yellow to cut."

He accompanies me to my noontime table and says good-bye. He's going to Sicily for the harvest of the little tomatoes, the cherry tomatoes.

I tell him he follows the earth.

"I follow your earth," he says, laughing. "It runs with the seasons while mine stands still."

In his gray hair there's a little yellow pollen, the mimosa showing its affection.

And in his hand he has red to drink in a glass cup, set against the white of his fingernails. Selim looks good in the company of colors. I think: this is what elegance is.

Then he dips his bread and says, "Travel overseas has led to good encounters. The American potato found olive oil and the tomato ended up on wheat."

He chews with relish as I think of his dark back bent over the red-green of the tomato plants, in the sun that rides on your shoulders ten hours a day, earning only half the fair rate. Finally I tell him that it is an honor for me to be at the same table.

I careen back and forth on the evening train, after an afternoon burdened by one glass too many.

At home I bite into raw garlic with tomatoes and a peeled boiled egg glows, for a moment, in the hollow of my hand.

Before my pupils roll back into sleep, I carry a thought to Laila. You eat roughly one spoonful of salt with a person and already you're in love. But before trusting each other, you should eat a kettleful of salt together.

Being with her is like life in Argentina, without a day after. In her arms I smell again the peat of Soledad Island.

I don't even know whether they're still searching for me on account of those years. The toy soldiers are no longer in command, but laws are odd and maybe they forget they're around, absentmindedly.

Who knows whether Maria has offered a bounty on my scalp or whether she's happy just to curse me.

I can't sleep. I get up to make coffee and look at the windows: in the distance, not even ten kilometers away, is the sea.

It was also night when I left Maria's island, climbing aboard a boat to climb back up to the parallels of return.

I take nothing away, only the money pocketed in exchange for ambergris, which is hidden beneath sheep manure to cover its hint of musk.

I vomit when the first waves hit. This is my only farewell.

We're working our way toward the equator's belly. The closer you get the less shadow your body leaves at noon.

I get stuck on a superstition, that a man without a shadow has no past.

For days and days I stand in the sun to watch it disappear.

I start all over again at the line where night is equal to day.

The sailors celebrate the crossing of the zero parallel. Rowdy nights on board, as the sea pushes from the stern into the long waves, the ship starts to descend.

The sailors sweat alcohol from their pores.

I'm a passenger, I mind my own business. But I break the nose of one guy who wants to have his way with the scullery boy, a Creole from the Antilles.

I do the wrong thing. Men should be left to their demons and there are places that aren't suitable for boys. And there are nights when men without women seek comfort in each other.

The boy races in front of me, the guy chasing him grabs him, he screams, and the only person around is me. That's how I get caught in the middle. The other guy pulls out a knife. I know what to do. I stick an elbow in his face and he goes down like the night.

So I spend the rest of the trip sleeping by day and staying on my feet at night so that I don't wake up with my throat cut.

The next day I have the captain give the knife back. He swears at me and grumbles that I shouldn't interfere.

I'm at a window on the other side of that world and that voyage. Yet just knowing that the straight line through the darkness goes to the sea is enough to give me another taste of Atlantic insomnia.

The first few nights I stay awake on the bridge to see the white of the moon on the water's smooth surface. If the sailor is thinking of slitting my throat, he'll wait for the nights when the moon is missing.

For days I cross paths with his glum, hungry face, his nose purple with blood that escaped from his veins.

I show him that I'm on my guard, that I fear him.

A small compensation, a satisfaction. Sometimes that's enough.

Out of gratitude, the boy wants to stay with me. He knocks on the cabin at night, brings me a slice of cake, a spiced coffee. There are men that lose their minds and their shame over boys. I can understand the men wanting boys, but not the other way around.

He tells me that the cook sold him to the sailor on equator night. And he says that no one has defended his body and his life since he was born. That he owes me everything, even love.

I already feel the air of the North. He is the South to which I had been so close in love, in war, and as a fugitive for twenty years. That South doesn't exist for me anymore.

I tell him that his attentions are more thanks than I deserve and that love has nothing to do with debts.

He asks if he can come with me when we land in England.

I don't know what I'll live on, I don't know anything about the North, how to get by, but if he's tired of the sea he can come with me.

He asks to hear a yes.

"Yes."

Now I'm thinking that Laila and I still don't have a yes or a no behind us. And you can't be two without a yes or a no.

After one hundred parallels of latitude, we descend into an upside-down world.

The landing place is London, and we get by. I work at a carpentry shop, he works evenings at a bar. He comes home and I'm asleep. In the morning he gets up to start my coffee, so we can welcome in the day together.

On Sundays we walk in the parks. We hear music from the South.

He asks me, "If I was a woman, would you marry me?"

Some nights he doesn't come home. He's started to work at a better bar. He has a proposal from a man to move in with him.

I tell him that the time has come for me to try my hand at Italy again. He accompanies me to the train the night I depart.

For the last time he removes a little sawdust from my head. Only at that point do I realize that I love his attentions to me, that I allow it by leaving in that sprinkle of dust from the shop.

I smile at myself for stopping at the surface of things, for not even understanding my pact with his attentions.

With his thumb he makes the sign of the cross on my forehead and says, "Find love for yourself."

"And make the men respect you. You're a loyal boy. You have dark eyes that don't know how to hide."

We say good-bye and each of us turns around and slips into the crowd of unknowns that surrounds every farewell.

And now I think I have to stop losing people.

The window mists over from peering into it and I lean my forehead against the touch of his cross from a remote place in the world, more than one year later, I call out wishing him a good night.

DAYS GO BY WITHOUT Laila.

I read a letter from Argentina, a friend got out of prison just recently. The world of my years in the South is cutting its last teeth.

He writes, "I have to learn to walk in a straight line, I have to understand that feet take you away."

The world mends on one side and on another it creates another twenty years of trouble.

I finish reading his letter at my table in the tavern. I fold it and close my eyes for a while.

"What's the man doing, sleeping?" Mimmo's voice opens my eyes. "Welcome back."

"No, I'm not sleeping, this letter has me thinking. I'll give it to you."

He sits down. Behind him is a woman. I only see her now. I apologize, stand up, introduce myself. She smiles and puts a little charm in her voice.

We all sit. He reads. I explain the letter to the woman: the release of a friend from a South American prison.

"Good news," she says.

Mimmo gives me back the letter. He asks me why I put stones in the vineyard. "What good is a rambling path between the rows?"

"It's not for walking," I reply. "The stones absorb sunlight during the day and release it at night. In summer the warmth lifts the night-time dew off the grapes and keeps them from spoiling."

He asks where I learned that.

"In the Argentina of my youth. The older Italians back then knew how to make wine in the gardens of Argentina. Now there are no longer any old or young Italians. Now they're all Argentineans.

"An old man, a grandfather without grandchildren, teaches me. He's been in Argentina ever since they cut down his woods back in the Apennines to make railroad ties. He fled from a world that erases centuries from the mountains to place them under railroad wheels.

"At night he hears the cloven forest crying out to the stars for revenge. When the locomotive boiler explodes they blame the anarchists. He flees from that world. He brings with him a small limestone mortar and a beechwood pestle to make pesto, some basil seeds and a bundle of Erbaluce vines with which he tries to grow a pergola in the humidity of the Palermo quarter in Buenos Aires."

The woman listens to me carefully. To her they must be fairy tales. Even Mimmo doesn't mind being quiet.

So I continue. "Nonno teaches me to take apart a pig. He works salt into it on an old willow plank, puts in garlic, pepper, and wine when needed. And as soon as the animal's throat has been cut, he collects the hot blood and fries it until it's spongy, and eats it for strength in his work, which has to be completed in a day."

She is repelled. I don't tell her, but not even I can swallow the stuff. No one can. But if you want a place among the elders you have to repeat one of their customs, from their youth, even a simple dance step on a feast day if you really can't stand to dip your bread in their soup.

I don't tell this to the woman and I fall silent. She stares at my forehead and says: "Again."

I remember Nonno talking about Indian women and how when the storm winds blow they go out bare-breasted to stop them.

I remember Nonno rubbing into his eyelids the first violet that came up after the winter. Then I say no more.

Mimmo tells me about himself.

He's coming back from a long trip along one of the borderlines of the war between Croatians and Serbians.

Two Italians, who knows how, brought a bread oven, a nice piece of machinery, to a tiny little town on the front.

Some of our guys can manage to slip themselves in anywhere, he says. "I met an old Croatian who for a long time was a factory worker in Austria. He's one of our guys from the old days, the kind that knows how to fix a car, making the spare parts himself, and then how to make cheese and wine."

The woman is standing there, magnificent. In silence she leans her chin against her fists. This already makes her alluring. She offers her ear, desire and time.

For a while I look at her as Mimmo says, "Eight children, the youngest shot in the head in the front yard, a shot that singed his hair, fired at close range."

The old man tells Mimmo how attractive war can be at the beginning. Debts, robberies, loans, contracts: war burns up every piece of paper. For some it's like an amnesty, for others a chance at revenge.

Then houses start to burn with the children inside and everyone loses.

Four years of war in that little town. The vineyard he planted is still filled with mines and the grapes of summer explode like the nipples of unmilked cows. The flies get drunk on them.

In winter he prays to the snow to bury the earth and

then prays to the frost to make the ground hard enough so he can walk on top and do the pruning.

The surrounding fields are still, the land mines waiting for footsteps.

"How can children grow up surrounded by so much forbidden land?" the woman asks, wanting no answer.

Mimmo leaves a little empty space after the woman's voice, to take it in.

He answers that the women tie their children up when they go out and have to leave them alone.

The woman knows about me, about Argentina, from something Mimmo said. She's young but not a girl and asks for an answer: whether I think I was useful.

A practical adjective. I like her saying it, but it has nothing to do with me. "You stay in the war because it would be shameful to stay out of it. And then grief seizes you and holds its grip till anger has turned you into a soldier."

"I wish I knew more," she says.

"I can only talk about it bluntly, without giving any explanation as to the why. My feeling is that it's not up to me but to someone who comes later, if he feels like it, and goes looking out of curiosity and pity. I don't feel like it."

"I can't understand why you don't give the 'why' of your story. To me already having a story seems so great that forgoing the why is a waste."

"I forgo it because so many lost lives sound like a justification of the why, an excuse. I don't know how to make excuses."

"It's a shame. I know other guys like you who fought and don't talk anymore, don't answer. You keep your reasons in your body."

"That's how it is," I say, she won't be alone, while Mimmo regrets the edge of rebuke in her voice. "That's how it is, we don't know how to behave in front of a question. We're the leftovers of a reply." We, I say, and I don't know who else I'm putting inside this jar of "we."

I swallow saliva and drown my voice in my throat.

Mimmo steps in to help me, says that a bit of explanation did come out of me.

"No, Mimmo, it's not good enough for her, only for me. And to you I say I am in your debt." And I bring my glass up to sip, slowly empty it, dry my mouth, and this means that for me the conversation is over.

We stand up, shake hands.

In the afternoon I have to brush the tree trunks with lime milk. This way I can tell Mimmo that tonight the moon is out and if he comes by, he can see a forest of ghosts.

Days go by working in another garden. I have to dig up a pavement of bulky, rough stone, bring the soil back to light and work it into planting soil. It's only a hundred square yards, but it's set solid. The stones are stuck to a cement slab and wire grid.

Blow by blow I have to break it with an iron sledgehammer. I sweat, smash my knuckles and fingers. Salt streams from my body.

I console myself with honey and strong cheese.

Under the crust of pavement the soil is spent, exhausted by darkness, scorched by lime. It needs oxygen and light. The salt absorbed has to be corrected with acidic loam.

For days I keep heaving the sledgehammer and the ash handle shakes with every blow. When I pick up a regular rhythm, I'm able to get a good look at myself from outside my body. From inside I feel the blows and labored breathing: inhale when I raise the iron, exhale when I bring it down on the stone.

The body's small bellows divides the movement into five beats: two to raise the sledgehammer, one suspended in the air, two to crash it down to earth.

From outside my body, I see a fifty-year-old man knocking at the gates of the earth to break it down, to smash gravel into its padlocked womb.

In a corner, I pile scrap metal twisted with cement chunks, then I load it onto a truck that carries it away.

In the end, I'm on uncovered land.

It's gray, I turn it over by the shovelful, enrich it with horse manure and chestnut mulch. I spread it out in combed columns in a late winter sun that embraces the whole and ferments it.

Days alone, working. Evenings at home, crushing raw tomato and oregano over a colander and peeling garlic cloves in front of a Russian book. It takes the weight off my body.

This is what books should do: Carry a person and not be carried by him; take the day off his back, not add its own ounces of paper to his vertebrae.

Late at night, Laila is a puff of my garlicky breath on the edge of sleep.

I also think about Selim who prays at every fare-well to the day. There are acts of humility that make a man great.

I go back to working in Mimmo's garden. I find a note from him: A woman came looking for me and he had to make a point of not giving her my address.

It's Laila. I think that I'll call her tonight. Instead she bursts into the tavern at noon, half angry, half glad, a shaken mass of freshly washed hair, maybe still wet.

She breathes words into my face, a tickling at the corner of my eyes. "You think it's funny?" She protests and then smiles.

She doesn't want to sit, so I stand. Two days she's been looking for me. She's furious and happy. She should kick me and kiss me, she says. She tears off hunks of bread to eat. "It's not my hand," I say.

"You'll see what I'll do to your hand and to the rest when no witnesses are around." And she insults me, swallows, turns around to leave, and orders me to come to her place after work without going home first and then she's off. So I sit and feel cramps in my stomach. I know my body loves this woman. It tells me by calling and gnawing at me.

I have to obey its braying, even if it means plodding after its tail.

I brush the palm of my hand, a rasp, over my face, I address my mind: We're not equal, you're an ancient skeleton, I'm the last of your tenants and I'm slow.

You balk like Balaam's ass when it sees the first angel. Unlike Balaam, I'm not your master and I don't raise the stick to force you to keep going. I owe it to you because of the burden placed and the risk and even because of your unswerving patience.

I take my hand from my face and place it on my esophagus to reach an understanding. If the body loves Laila, then so do I. This calms the nerve that had snapped at her arrival, after her voice and sudden, perfumed disappearance.

Sometimes to take two steps in a row, one after the other, I need to write a contract with myself.

At Laila's place there's happiness. She even has flowers on.

"What fertilizer do you use to make them so beautiful?" I ask, and touch one of the painted flowers on her dress.

"You're the gardener, guess."

I have to move things around below and sniff. I place my finger between her skin and the fabric of her neckline. "What's the idea of wearing a flowered dress, to attract bees and gardeners?"

I withdraw my finger and breathe on top of it, pretending it's burnt. And we start off with jokes before plunging into hugs.

Young people make absorbed, concentrated faces in love, older people are more playful and warm their blood with laughter. Laughter impels.

The water is boiling but we don't put in the pasta.

When we go back to the kitchen, an inch of very salty water is still resisting on the open flame. "Like the waters of the Dead Sea," she says.

We're hungry, so we fry six eggs and sop them up with bread straight from the pan, face to face, she with the soft part, me with the crust.

She eats more than me. I don't know how to swallow quickly.

I pour one of her wines, French, the kind that makes the palate genuflect. I have no mouth for such delicacies. She does, and she swishes it in her mouth and cradles it. I toss back half a glass in a second.

"With those passages through the mouth, you'll end up spitting it out." She rocks with laughter while swallowing and some goes down the wrong way so she really does end up spitting it out. She punches me in the arm and then hacks up a wild red.

Fried eggs were my survival plate once I'd left home, the discovery that I could cook. Nothing but fried eggs, for the first few months.

We put the pan away without washing it because it's been deep cleaned by the bread slices.

"You do the talking, Laila, don't make me tell stories."

"I was a dentist, I have steady hands. I can read a root's humor even without X-rays. I grip it with the forceps and know which way to twist to extract it right."

I look at the joints in her hand, understanding its agility and grip, a force that comes more from the back of the hand than the palm. I know hands better than faces.

She's no longer a dentist. One day by mistake she makes an incision beneath a canine into an artery in the palate. The man's mouth fills with blood in two seconds. She is able to stop it, to close it, but decides to quit the profession. It's just an accident, ended well, but she quits anyway.

I ask if my mouth is healthy.

"Yes," she says, "yours is full of air, a dark cellar, a cave in the sandstone filled with silence."

On my tongue I taste the cork and my teeth are bits of gravel consumed by chewing, by bread.

"There are many kinds of mouths," she says, "gutter mouths that spew saliva and empty words, marsupial mouths that always hold a sleeping puppy, mouths of sealed envelopes never mailed."

She speaks without hands, just lips.

She asks if I work with my shirt on even in the summer, because the sun's marks stop at my neckline.

"Yes," I say, "a working man wears darkened skin on his face, neck, and hands. The rest is on vacation."

She laughs, I don't know why.

She has an egg smear that I brush away with my thumb. She presses her mouth against it to start. Our naked feet rub beneath the table. We're lovers who hold each other's feet rather than hands. We put our arms around each other. I'm a little tense, she's relaxed, no murky shadows in her tenderness like a scirocco that hurls the laundry into the air.

Working girls have a repertory. When they love, they avoid it and circle it through familiar gestures without falling in, sidestepping it automatically. They invent love in the midst of sacrifices, of bans on acting "as if."

In Laila's hands, love is the most virginal flesh. She seeks it by calling its name on her breath. She calls to me from outside of her openness.

Finally her embrace gathers my blood and she is fulfilled by the reserves still left in me.

She says it's nicer for her when I'm tired.

And I know from the start that I love this woman and that this love has the right to be my last.

It's night and our feet intertwine again. The rest of the body has broken away.

I think of an island where you go barefoot, an island after Laila, when the time has come to leave terra firma. I need an island after her, after my feet are untied from hers.

"What are you thinking?" she asks, just to hear me say it.

"Of an island, of waves breaking against cliffs, of a wind that lets the trees grow, of well water and a gutter that carries the rainwater to it. I'm thinking of a pulley sighing over the well and the water humming at the bottom and of the peace that comes from having some water in reserve."

Then I make up things that I can say after "I'm thinking of."

"You've got a good imagination," she says.

"Yes, like a man who shaves without a mirror."

Laila listens to me and is so close to my ear that she breathes inside the island.

Except that I don't tell her it's a place for the time after her. Love is a one-way ticket and afterward there's no taking shelter in the earlier room.

"I like the silly accuracy in the things you say. I ask you what you're thinking and you give yourself an island, a well and even a rainpipe. I get emotional seeing you discombobulated. I think this is *izvestie* of love, news of love." She corrects herself like her Russian grandmother, who could mix different languages in the same sentence.

I notice news of love as well. My body holds on to Laila's words about the pleasure gleaned from my tiredness, and rejoices with gratitude. This is news of love.

"Tomorrow I have something to tell you," she says.

"Why not now?"

"No, tomorrow, now it's late but tomorrow night yes, no hugging, just some serious talk for a little while."

"Yes, a little while," I say, "because if you don't laugh afterward I'll be sick." Our feet rub against each other to say good night.

IN THE GARDEN I burn the laurel trimmings, a scent that invites your eyes to shut.

From behind the gate Selim's coalman face returns. I invite him into the shed. "You're the spirit of coffee," I tell him, "you appear when I'm about to put it on the flame."

"I can smell it for miles, before you've even thought about it," he says, seriously.

We sit down, I ask him about the harvest. Good work but half of his earnings were robbed at knifepoint, only half was sent home. Four guys with knives, for a small amount that, divvied up, didn't give them enough for a Saturday night on the town.

"Who would rob a laborer?" I ask.

"Boys without need," he says.

"Does it hurt?"

"The shame comes from your feelings, not from an injury," he says.

Then Selim drinks his coffee sitting next to me in front of the burning twigs.

With a remaining branch he pokes at a corner. "The ashes say that you have to leave."

He says it so softly that I can only hear it thanks to the dry, smoking silence.

I look at the shifted embers that hum with a whispering of oak, like Laila's voice, but rather than make me speak they want me to listen.

I'm initially annoyed by this earthen horoscope from downcast black eyes. I swallow, saying only that I have no place I'm trying to reach. "Here no one is following me and no one is waiting for me elsewhere."

"You have to leave."

"I don't leave anymore. Now my verb is to stay. There's also a woman to love."

"The ashes see blood, including yours shed beside it. The ashes don't say love."

"The ashes don't know my business."

Selim pokes at another spot, flips, strews, looks me in the eyes and says with a vein that fills his forehead: "Me too."

I don't know what part of my life he's meddling in, but I believe him. I think maybe one of his ancient hours equals one of mine. If so, then all the more reason to be friends.

"This is not the only thing. We also have an hour that matches up in the future," and his voice dies down with the last flames of the kindling.

"Don't tell, Selim, let's stick to some future coffee instead and let ashes be ashes. If they're mad at me it's because not long ago they were still green fiber and alive."

"You care for the trees and they love you back. These are their words to you, their last."

"Do you know anyone who departs on the advice of trees, Selim?"

"You do," he says, "I do. I left because of the ashes from a vultures' nest."

"But I'm the last to leave, the one that clears the table and closes the door."

"There are many signs," he says, "they arrive with leaves, birds, raindrops. Ashes are the last advice."

I keep silent, finish drinking from the cup.

Selim's voice is quiet, it already comes from afterward, from a time that follows the present. He sniffs at the wind and smoke and says: "We are friends, *làzima kuwa rafiki*, we have to be friends." He shifts the ashes, erases.

Holy man of Africa, I think, you come to impart your wisdom to a European savage who follows the moon on the calendar and the clouds on the radio bulletin and can't read a word without an alphabet.

"Is life so in tune, so musically scored as to notify through signs, counterpoints? Better to know nothing ahead of time. Because it takes your kind of patience to bear the knowledge. It takes your wide nose, your teeth shining through to smile, your forehead furrowed with sweat. It takes your calloused gray and not my eggshell color."

Selim finishes his cup and mumbles his syllables of benediction.

"You're familiar with ashes and the sky, you know so many things, Selim."

"I only breathe out a few thank yous to the heavens," he says. "I make my breath rise. It mixes with the clouds and becomes rain. A man prays and in this way builds his substance in the sky. The clouds are filled with the breath of prayers."

I look above, the clouds are arriving from the sea. I say, "Man how they pray in Sardinia!"

And he laughs with me and says that it's good to laugh and that faith comes after laughter rather than after tears.

Then he stands up. In the depths of my empty intestines, agitated by the coffee, I feel a growling of tenderness for Laila, who has landed on my fifty years like a stone on a nest.

I haven't been home for a day, I think, while cleaning the coffeepot.

Skip a turn and you never return. In Argentina I miss an appointment and I'm safe. I arrive just as they're taking away the family from the last hiding place. I stay in the bus, which is blocked by soldiers, while my last friends disappear into a truck.

The ashes can't teach me anything, Selim. I am the ashes.

Selim makes a bouquet of rosemary branches and thyme. He wants to try selling them to restaurants. Now that they're in bloom they can be set on tables instead of vases.

He thinks that good business requires items that no one has asked for yet. The demand has to be invented. This way he feels like he's offering a novelty.

"How does the idea come to you?" I ask.

"I look at gardens. There are many new items in gardens. But there are not many gardeners," and he makes a smile that uncovers his teeth.

And I think that the most important thing at his and my age is maintaining your smile.

I strew the ashes over the loose soil surrounding the oak that I've planted. I can't help but say a couple of words. I pat the still delicate trunk. There's already a robin on one of its branches. Selim's voice saying goodbye from the gate arrives from behind, together with the sun that is already warming my back. I unbutton the collar of my red flannel shirt and pull up the sleeves. I've been wearing it for two days. It's filled with my smell like the book I keep in the pocket of my overalls.

At the tavern I sit at my usual place, which has a good view of the front door.

For the first time I find myself looking up each time someone comes in. Selim's news, the warning of the ashes, has given half a twist to my nerves. The first sign is my vigilance. I don't like it and I have to be careful to keep my body from trembling.

A narrowing of the eyelids reminds me of a lesson learned from Argentina, from quick glances, a heavy jacket and hot breath running through my nose. And my hand starts to make a lost gesture and I realize that it's resting on the spot left empty by the weapon of my years in the South. Before regaining control of my nerves, I sense this groping in search of a lost object.

And it's a long time before I can take a deep breath, unwinding.

The tavern-keeper comes up and sits down. He's got his walnut liquer and pours me a glass.

"What are you thinking about, my friend? A woman?"

"No," I say, and feel my narrowed eyelids relax and a hint of a smile slowly arise. "I'm thinking of a town in the South, of many years down there."

"You still haven't realized that you're back, have you."

"Here I do. At your place it's like being in an old-fashioned house, open to everyone. Is there something to celebrate?" I ask.

"Yes," he says, "a birthday of sorts. On this day many years ago I got out of prison."

He touches his glass against mine. "Welcome out," I say and he says, "Welcome home."

I toss the walnut liquer down my throat and start on the road uphill to the garden. I set my heel more forcefully into my step and Argentina abandons my thoughts.

As work ends it's still light out. Laila is waiting for me at the gate. She doesn't want to talk indoors. We go down to the sea.

The wisteria is beginning to bloom on the path to the beach from where we leave the car. I take my shoes off. I walk more in touch with the ground than with Laila's first words. We sit on stones. The light arrives at an acute angle that narrows and beckons far from the struggling words.

I listen to her and think of the ruckus of soldiers fumbling through the rocks in search of me. I know I'll have to come out into the open.

Laila speaks of a man to kill or be killed.

Her job is to make men talk. She's had enough. "The last trip took a lot out of me. It took me a long time to finish, I couldn't. I had the imprint of your hands on me, all over me. It took me days, nausea, nostalgia, and now I know it's over. I can't take anymore. He's onto me, is watching me, is already setting up another date and I'm trying to find time I don't have. This is not the kind of job you're allowed to quit. When you can't do it anymore, you either run away or die."

I barely listen, thinking of Dvora, the Buenos Aires girl who I followed down there, of our good years, the Sundays when I wake her by slipping a drop of jasmine under her nose to see her smile in her sleep. And meanwhile the crowds pass through the streets with banners and from our balcony it looks like bunches of grapes, the fruit is their heads, and at the beginning we never think that the crowd belongs to us, singing the serenade of its reasons to us onlookers.

The crowd parades below and we stay on our balconies, in a kind of accompaniment. And some people from below wave for us to come down and I want to wave to everybody to come up, to reciprocate, and meanwhile I greet them with my eyes and don't realize that Dvora has gone down to the street. She waves to me and shows me the way and then so do I. It only lasts one year and the bad times come in one day, when they throw her into a car and pull me away by force and there I am doubled over from the sobs in the street like a crooked nail. I'm safe, discarded by death because of the green Italian passport in my pocket. "Where have I brought you, *novio*? Here they'll kill us all."

And her eyes cloud up and I rub my finger over her eyelids and tell her, "Hey, why the teardrops?" And these are the last words and the last caress at the gate, before being separated by death.

I leave our family home. I enter the vagabond war where every shelter is an artificial home. From our wedding house I take away only one thing of Dvora's, her sneakers, still tied tight because she takes them off by pulling on the heel. It's my job to untie the knots and keep them ready for her. I carry them away, out of my mind with pain, to remind me of a debt of neglected care, in the hope of seeing them on her feet again.

Then I forget them and a year later I have to empty out one of my underground shelters and I find them again under a purse in the back of a closet. I have nothing of Dvora's because without her I am grasping onto nothingness. Her shoes are there with the laces tied tight. I kneel down and loosen the knots, the eyelets. Then I leave them there.

I know that she's at the bottom of the sea with her hands tied. I can only untie her shoelaces. I bid farewell on my knees before an empty closet.

I think of this beneath Laila's words and once more nothing of me is left.

In the suburb to the south of the Palermo quarter in Buenos Aires I run into the last survivors of the first Italians who arrived. I work in a shoe factory, learn about leather and enjoy the love of Sundays on Dvora's arm with the promise of growing old and foolish together.

I don't have a death-rattle of regret for the shootings, the little war, the portion of revenge taken without paying. Because I'm unharmed: I don't know how to say it, don't know how to curse it.

I'm barely listening, Laila, a short return by way of cruel Argentina. It's better not to be in a room right now, better to see an arm of the Mediterranean than the immense mouth of the Rio de la Plata.

Laila isn't asking for help, she's speaking out of loyalty, like the first time. She wants to shrug off her problems. I believe her.

I join my empty palms. I think: Now you, too, with the killing?

My hands stay closed as do my words. I say nothing. Instead Laila says, "Me, too, with the killing."

She hears my inner rumblings. I don't react, don't have a single sentence I can keep secret from her. It must be really uncomfortable to listen to thoughts, fill yourself with other people's chaos even when they're silent. It's tough to know that, while you're speaking to a guy, he is thinking of something else.

The sea is purple, like the rosemary flower. The wind of the last rays of sun blows Laila's hair over my forehead.

"So that's how you snatch my thoughts, with your hair?"

"No," she says. It's an animal ability, a remnant of the brain of a snake, a fish, a swallow, or at least that's what she imagines her gift to be. But she can only hear thoughts that are close by.

Doesn't this scare me? Nothing scares me about this love.

She hugs my arm and says, "You make me forget who I am."

"No, I help you to know better. You are the woman I am in love with. For me no reason could be better."

"You caress every bone in my body, place your lips on my marrow, set my body at peace," she says.

Her hair whips my face, wants to place itself downwind. No, I hold it, I don't want her hair to blow aimlessly.

We are quiet for a while, tasting the salt on the dying wind.

"It's disgusting to kill, Laila. You never get rid of death's grease. It doesn't wash away. You're young, so you think that it will pass and through a fit of willpower for a while you do forget it. And then one day when you're at peace with the world and are looking at it and feel the air teasing your breath and are maybe thinking of the tiny bit of oxygen and the huge amount of nitrogen, the furthest point from that bloodshed, it comes back because you, yes you, are breathing, living, you're one of the damned living.

"And you recite the most urgent reasons for the bloodshed and you repeat that, at night you sleep and every sleep contains absolution, and no matter, the murdered one is still there, attached to you.

"And remorse doesn't count and you don't have to get insomnia, but there you are surrounded by empty seats, a woman changes sidewalks when she runs into you, bread crumbles in your hands, faces that resemble, annoyance at hearing footsteps at your back and, at the first stroke of luck, the thought that you, too, might end up mowed down by bullets and have no right to dodge them.

"And when you admit this, you actually feel relief.

"So many murderers let themselves be killed."

And I continue, I continue reading to Laila an awkward lover's plea.

"Otherwise he'll kill me. Because I don't want to continue anymore and as a free woman he thinks I'm a danger. And he knows about you and this is making things risky for you."

"I don't know how to shield you from evil. It's the second time I've failed, but the first I went about it numbly and reacted late and for revenge. Now that I've wasted half a lifetime running away, I still cannot save anyone."

"You can't pull me out of the water dry. I'll serve him as long as I can and not even that is sure to satisfy him. One day he'll decide that someone knows too much and, pity because she was good, but it's better to get rid of the problem.

"I used to think I could stick it out, now it's impossible to stick it out and leave it at that. And I'm ending up straight in the mouth of one of the quick fixes. You rattled me just in time, through a couple of wrinkles on the neck, a way of crumbling sage and scenting your fingers, the quiet silence that sits in your thoughts. Now I have to save myself. To kill and escape and this way have a few days' advantage over people who know about me while I know nothing about them."

Who are they? I try to imagine without asking.

"They're people quick to do harm. You already know some of them."

"You need help, that's what I'm saying."

"No, and the less you know the better."

"They might come looking for me."

"I don't know, it's not for sure. They work by sector, maybe he's still the only one that knows about you. Whatever the case you won't be able to say anything. I'm not telling you how to get in touch with me."

"It ends here, Laila." While I'm saying this my eyes go dry. I touch the book in my pocket for support, feel a wind from other waves on my brow. It's the Atlantic from the South, flight and fury inside my body to avoid getting caught by the Argentinians who come ashore to occupy Soledad Island.

It's April, autumn. I run away from Maria without saying a thing. She's one of them and once again I'm in the land of hunt and capture.

I hide by a coastal inlet on a tip of the island called "Eagle's Pass," the southernmost tip, tempests and marine birds and winds that ruin your ears.

I fish, drink rainwater, steal eggs from nests, make peat fires at night and feel the trap snapping at me from every side. I resist, just enough to live. I discover the carcass of a sailboat, salvage wood from it for my hiding place in the grotto.

I spend days in hiding, looking out at the sea.

I feel my life hardening to absorb the blow and accept it.

There's no escape at land's end, no other South where I can descend, no ship's hold where I can rock in a sleep of salvation.

I see the sea scratching the cliffs and the white of the waves' nails and the line that separates it from the land.

I see the thin red line of sunset that separates day from night, I think that the world is made by the king of the verb "divide," and I wait for the line that comes to detach me from the days.

And life is a long-spun line and death is going back to the start, bodiless. I see the thrashing of wings inside the hollow of waves and not even a fish with the whole ocean to hide in is safe.

The birds fly above: each is alone and unallied. Their family is the air, not the wings of others, and each egg laid is solitude. And in the darkness of embers I make an omelet of solitude and kill my hunger.

And when the feeling grabs me that my time is near, I think of what is streaming through most of the world and passing alongside mine: trees ruffling pollen, women waiting for water to break, a boy studying a verse of Dante, a thousand recess bells ringing in every school on earth, wine fermenting in casks. Everything is happening together with me so time joins with these forces to become something more.

Thoughts of a life gone by, Laila, I know you are listening to them.

It lasts several weeks. They find me by combing the area
and I escape over the cliffs, they fire against the wind and
a lead pebble goes through my lungs and I think I can see
it coming out the front and escaping even further ahead,
with me running behind it until my breath stops. Finally
my ears are becalmed and I hear them kicking like they were
at a gate. One guy wants to do me in right there and then
and the others say sending me to the mainland will make a
better impression. They put me in the back of a truck like
an animal after the hunt and circle the city shooting in the
air saying that they've captured a terrorist and they call me
the *aparecido* and throw me in prison. An English doctor
sews up the exit and entry points and tells me good luck
and to hang in there, his guys are on their way.

I don't know who his guys are, but after a few nights
I hear cannons at sea.

And I'm on the cot in my cell and no more guards are
around and from other cells they're screaming with hunger, no food for days. Then they come to open the cells
and everyone is crazy with joy and I can't breathe, but I
know that death is spitting in my face once again.

All these stories are just an inch away from Laila's
head. Once again there's no time and we have to arrange

another night for leaving each other. We break away from the dark sea. I slip on my shoes and slip one arm under hers.

"Until the last of us remains, I will stay," I tell Laila.

"Let's go to a room," she says, "get right into making love. I don't want to waste that lucky bullet that exited without killing."

We go to my little neighborhood, on the outskirts of the sea. At the windows the eternal laundry drips and from the balconies the short-sleeved arms of women shake.

The kitchen air is withering. I open the windows. In comes the strangled shout of a courtyard game of soccer. Laila looks out, then she opens drawers, finds the corkscrew and from her handbag comes a bottle. While I'm putting the glasses on the table, the buzzing of her voice begins. I recognize it, try to stop it with my hand, she holds it in the air and again I hear my words taking leave of me.

I see them even as I say them.

"There's a house on an avenue hedged in bougainville. Inside is a man wearing a uniform and on the street another waiting to shoot. There's a minimal escort, a driver. When he comes out I emerge from the hedges with the advantage of being fast, alone. In my mouth I clench the reins of my nerve ends. And a radio starts up with a song. The moment is filled with musical notes, I stress them all, the seconds jump like tarantella steps and I see the side of a uniform and a hand that searches for a weapon too late and the driver tries something then dashes for cover. I jump into his car and take off and hear a few shots go off, but mainly I hear the song on the car radio that's still on."

How can I be spitting out another cursed hour? You see, I've stopped talking and started to sing that song on the radio. While I'm singing, the buzzing sound from Laila's close-lipped voice comes to a stop. I sing and the story stops, I sing and there's nothing to obey and once again I'm inside my own voice.

And Laila says that I'm the first to break free on his own and she is happy not to have this hold over me. "Songs are what loosen and release you from my sound. Now you know." And she says that this, too, is a sign of her stopping.

"You don't have this hold over me," I say. "You have something more. You took a bite. With you I'm bitten like a piece between two jaws, you have a hold on me, I let myself be held because you want me and I can't find anyone in the world who knows how to want a person, how to spend all this desire."

"I want you," she says, "and it's up to you to open your arms and hold me. I love you out of love and out of disgust with men. I love you because you're whole even if you are left over from another life. I love you because the piece that remains is worth the whole and I love you by exclusion of the other lost pieces."

We stay still, drink her picnic wine. I cut hard cheese, sprinkle some sage and a sliver of oil.

She eats with strong jaw movements, chewing a lot, swallowing slowly, sniffing the smell of the room.

I already have basil in different pots, making this a field of smells.

She takes a walnut, places it on my palm. I put it on the table and open it with a little smack against my forehead, a game that amuses the children in the courtyard when I do it at the window.

Laila laughs. "The Americas," she says, "made you loco."

Turning serious, she asks if a person could plan an assault with no escape route, whether he had to be off his rocker or just determined to let himself be killed while killing.

"It's America of the South, Laila, days without a day after. Not many people are left. You barrel around like a soul unhinged. You face down blows without bending, since it's not up to you whether you live. You stick it out. We're fish on the surface of the water."

Don't ask me, Laila, I think. I'm not that man anymore, no one can stay that way for long. That's why wars end and a later generation catches its breath looking forward and erasing what's behind. Escape route, you say. I remember the escape but not the route. I'm lost and I run to the bottom of Argentina, I don't stop anymore.

I run over the scorched plains of the South where you can be seen for miles. No one would go hunting there.

I'm seeking the bottom, the void.

I feel hidden by the wind that squeezes your eyes shut and puts your ears to sleep.

At night I walk along the side of the road. If a light appears on the horizon's funnel, I lay on my back behind a bush.

At dawn I leave the road and stretch out to sleep, far away.

One day a goat wakes me, it wants to be milked. I empty it, drink the best milk of my life.

I spend a few days with the goat, step-by-step, eye-to-eye.

I forget. I look at it and forget.

It sleeps next to me, at dawn it licks my nose.

I give it a little of my salt ration. We drink at a lost underground river. We climb back up.

From the distance I see a fence. The goat goes toward it. I turn around and return.

I spend a day picking off fleas in the bend of a river. I search my clothes for lice like towns on a map. I wash, smack, dry.

I learn not to fear snakes, wise creatures that lick the air.

In two days I find the road again. I go back to walking south at night.

I trust the darkness, bare my pupils, align my thoughts.

One night in the distance I notice a campfire on the road. I take a downwind approach, to avoid giving a scent to any dog possibly nearby. I listen to voices, two Italian mountain climbers with a broken car.

I wait for the dawn, show myself, introduce myself as an Argentinian wanderer. They explain the problem, I understand and fix it. I get a ride and a soup. It's been more than a month since I've eaten anything hot. My stomach rumbles a nursery rhyme like the foliage of a tree when the nests reawaken.

They ask me nothing. I listen to their intricate projects, a new scaling line up a granite pillar behind the last ridge of walls in the world. They talk to each other seriously and intently, about this and this alone. They have just enough money. They've been traveling for a week, following a map, looking straight ahead.

I can't remember ever having been like them. I listen to them like a stranger. They're men with only one side, facing forward without casting a single look back. They're men who don't turn around.

Stretched out on their rope coils, I feel the nerve

bundles in my back that make me move, turn around, go forward at the sound of footsteps.

I travel with men who don't watch their backs. All their risks are ahead of them. I listen to them and rest. The road down is now a question of wheels, maps, not soil and stars.

I look at the route on the map. For the first time I know where I am and the distance contained in my escape.

With an engine below, the place in the South I'm headed for is within a day's reach.

I fall asleep behind the best strangers, dangerous only to themselves. They have a straight line to follow. They tread an outline. I take advantage of their trail. For the first time I go in a straight line, but my escape is sketchy, like the folds in the wings of a bat.

It's evening when I suddenly ask to get out and say goodbye.

It's the road of a seaside town, I go to the port and brush a mooring cable with the back of my hand. I smell my childhood on the Mediterranean and try to look like a sailor when I shove a tavern door.

The room is smoky, the wind that sneaks in with me shakes it like a rag. A lamp throws light in the face of anyone who enters. "What are you looking for, mister?" asks a voice from behind a counter while I try to understand whether the place convinces me.

I lower my eyes and go calmly toward the voice, even if its welcome is a slap on my nerves.

I sit down, and tell him that I'm looking for a place to sleep and a passage.

"To travel or to work?"

Now that I'm not under the light anymore I can see the tavern-keeper, a hairless bear. I set my hands on the counter and get the urge to tell it like it is: that I'm not a sailor, but I can do any type of work to pay for the trip.

"Kid's stuff, you're too old to be a ship boy."

Now I look at him. I see eyes purple with exploded veins. He's at least sixty with hair as white as ice.

"A man's life lasts as long as three horses'. You have already buried the first."

"I've got a little money and I can wait," I say.

"I don't think so. You're in a rush. You came to the counter too slowly."

"Can you help me?" I say. I don't know what's gotten into me to speak this way rather than walk out of there quickly with my gun at the ready to dissuade anyone from coming after me.

"Let me have a look at your hands," he says.

I open them up in front of him. They're dirty, steady. But he immediately turns them over, uncovers my wrists.

"There's still good stuff in you. I'll put you on a ship and you'll go away from here. You'll be safe. It'll cost you your children: you won't have any. Guys like you are left without any."

I'm about to spit in his face when I feel a cramp deep in my intestines and throw a hand on the countertop to grip something.

And he tells me in another low, low voice, that there's a bunkroom upstairs and a free bed. To stay there and not go out. For meals he would come to call me. I don't know why, but I do as he says. And I climb up to a big room and wash myself before tasting a bed for the first time since I fled. I keep my gun cocked, because if he gives me up to the police I want to be ready. On the brink of sleep I have a gloomy thought: that saving yourself is only pushing yourself even deeper into the trap rather than getting out. Dying is the only way out.

The tavern-keeper wakes me to eat his fish stew, at the counter. I pick at it with my hands, down to the last bones, then I gulp down the broth from the bowl.

I chew badly. My face is like pressed cardboard. It doesn't melt for food or even for a smile.

On the opposite wall is a map of the world. It's upside down, with Antarctica on top. He notices me staring at it.

"You're from the North," he says, "Northerners act so dumb when they see their nice planet upside down. For us instead that's the way the world is, with the South on top."

I sit there with my eyes lost on the map.

"Irish sailors come to fill their bladders with beer and they stare and move their heads like dogs when they sense something strange. You and your northern heads are blind. You only understand the earth when you turn it around the other way. Look at the continents: they all push toward the North and end up in that hemisphere. Because they broke away from Antarctica and are traveling toward the lower part of the planet, down where they plunge. They leave the oceans behind them. Even the sea currents start here in the South, because this is the beginning, the high point of the earth. And Antarctica is land, with mountains and volcanoes, not frozen water like your icicles. The North draws up false maps with its nice pole on the top. Truth is the North is at the bottom of the bag. Then all you care about is East and West, while for us they're just choppy water, westward and eastward oceans. We're at the pointed horn of the world, huddled close to the ground so that we won't be torn away by the wind."

I listen to him and believe everything he's saying, even the promise of a passage. An Irish fishing ship is supposed to arrive. He'll put me on it.

Host of the upside down, what a man. He sizes up a fellow with his eyes and turns maps around. I force myself to smile at him, but I don't know how to move my face anymore. My hands are greasy, I pass the back of my hand over my mouth to clean it but especially to rub it, to push it into a grin. I force my mouth to harden into the most stilted of smiles.

Then he pours me half a glass of cloudy bitter water. "My treat," he says, and I accept and feel it plunge into my chest like a knife and I paper my eyes to keep from spurting tears. It's liquid fire for a man who hasn't touched any degree of alcohol for years.

A stirring of cordiality, a being at peace before another man runs through my body. I deliver myself to this hairless bear who with the same hand could send me out to sea or break my spine. Who knows what it is about me that makes him decide one of the two.

The upside-down map looks right to me now. It teaches me how to stand on the antipode. The escape I thought was toward the bottom is turned upward. I'm at the peak of a cliff waiting to dive.

At night on a cot in the bunkroom I hear the bitter breath of marooned sailors looking for a berth, travelers waiting for a lucky voyage. We are men inside a hold that doesn't take to sea. No one speaks to the other. During the day they stand with their heads bent down, like sunflowers at night.

When the ship arrives he tells me, "Climb aboard when it's dark. Don't bring any weight, just your clothes. Throw the rest away, you won't need it anymore, ever again."

I do what he says.

Laila hugs me, pours wine, brings it to my lips. I keep my hands closed to hear the sounds of the neighboring families sitting down to supper.

She says she doesn't know anyone who talks about the past using the present tense.

"What am I supposed to do with verbal gymnastics? I'm not the master of time. I'm its beast of burden."

"It was alright for writers of the past and their once-upon-a-time."

"And the future tense helps fortune-tellers who grow rich on predictions. I know the lives that last a day. Making it to the night is already to die old. The future doesn't need verbs, it needs nouns. Mine is the word 'rain-pipe' that in an unknown well collects rainwater on a parched island."

"My future," she says, "is a dirty, practical little verb."

"To kill?" I ask. She puts her head down and takes her arms off my shoulders.

I say nothing.

Once that verb is used it stays in your body, forever.

A dewy freshness enters in. Voices from televisions seek to blare affection, the houses run under an electric regimen.

I close the windows, keep the lights off.

"I have no more power over you. Now you know how song is released from my voice. All it takes is a stanza to rouse you."

I couldn't break away even if I sang until morning like a blind finch. I go toward her, take her in my arms, circle the room, stop at the window and sing to her, "*E tu gondola, bella mia gondola, sulle mie braccia dondola do,*" and she swings inside the hammock of my arms.

"If you're the sea, then hold me."

I lay her out on the sheets.

We undress and hold each other naked without kisses.

This night is a shelter to cherish in the mind, not a wedding boat.

To stay with our heads leaning against each other, say the right words to plant affection and make sure it lasts.

She looks at me from atop an elbow propped on a pillow and places a finger over the scar left by the bullet that raced ahead of me. She says she'd like to find that bullet and wrap it around her finger like a wedding ring.

"I can't imagine living without you, gardener, even if I wring my imagination out. I can think coolheadedly about ambushes, about moving quickly so I get there before him. I can plan the details of the escape. But what I can't do is see beyond you."

"Laila, for you I am a steam-powered love, the force that moved the first trains, the first ships without sails."

"Steam-powered love is good for one era."

"You go through many and now you're in the early nineteen-hundreds. You have to wage your war and if you come back alive, then will come the electric loves, turbo-powered. You can't see them from here."

"The love I bring you is the kind that burns slowly, like a good wood- or coal-burning furnace. It's good for departures."

"Your thirty years have been still for a while."

"I believe your story, that you are risking defeat. And I believe your news, that you are somehow drawn to me. But I'm staying, you're going away, and my wish to you is that you come out on the other side of life, even if it is on the other side of the world."

"My steam-powered love, we'll look at unclouded days and, if I manage to live, I'll look for your rain-pipe island."

The day doesn't come; the night withdraws.

I know the exact point when. Everything is still a black pavement, then a paper rustles on the street, less than a single beat of a fan. Next to his wife, a man's hand soundlessly slips on a shoe in the dark. An old woman's head slumps while reading a novel, waiting for sleep to return. Suddenly the night draws together at one spot through a secret movement and the darkness is not a gas but an oil slithering off to the west.

I know the point in the night when it breaks away from the earth and slides away on top of it. However much a laborer who's been on his feet for some time already might wish it were day, there's still a part of him that wouldn't mind chasing after the night, to travel westward inside its darkness.

That's the spot where I break away from the sleep of Laila, who's ended up on my arm.

First she grabs my pillow as a trade-off, then she wakes. "It's my time," I say, "you can sleep." But she wants to leave the house with me, so she asks if we can clink coffee together.

In the half-spent kitchen lit by the corridor, we warm ourselves with a cup.

She rubs her nose and her slumber against my freshly shaven face. She exhales and swallows and ruffles her hair. Our good-bye feels like gunshots.

"Don't think of that now, I can hardly stand up."

You're half-asleep but you still hear my buzzing.

"Go ahead and sing, that way I don't hear anything."

I start to hum the gondola nursery rhyme and she punches me in the chest with a clumsy fist. "Not that one again or I'll faint," and she releases a yawn as long as the howling of a wolf.

She leans against me, we go out, the outside air is brisk. She grumbles, "What the hell kind of life do people lead who leave the house at this hour?"

"Laila, this is what the laborers of the world do. They get up before it's light, come home after it's light. They move from darkness to darkness."

Laila takes a deep breath, I don't know if she's exhaling or yawning.

Near us someone else is on his way, a guy I know. I offer him a ride in Laila's car. She throws herself in the back seat and huddles to catch up on her sleep.

The man says nothing, he's shy. He's going to a construction site, a corked bottle and faint smell of pasta coming out of his shoulder bag. His wife gets up before him to cook it and put it in his lunch-box. He works with iron, laying down the grid for pillars. He keeps his hands folded in his lap: two orange peels lined with broken capillaries.

I leave him at a bus stop.

Laila moves to the front, she's awake.

"I don't know when I'm going to do it, but it'll be soon. After that we'll manage to find each other somehow."

To hide my thoughts I start humming an old Christmas song of the *zampognari*. Laila laughs, then she immediately stops.

A car with a man inside is parked in front of the garden where I work. I don't need to ask if it's him. We're at a corner where we can see him without being seen.

In a hoarse voice I ask Laila brusquely to give me his address. I feel another twist on my nerves, up an octave. My feet are hot and my face is cold.

"Don't mess things up," she says.

I insist, bluntly.

She says a street, a number, I don't need to write it. I get out without touching her. I hear her shifting into reverse. I go back up the road. Before entering the garden I pass slowly next to the stopped car on the driver's side. We stare at each other and I feel salt in my mouth. One of us is already dead and now I don't care who.

I cross the street and go into the garden.

I need to check out the address. I think I'll go during my break.

Spring is ready. Inside their wood the trees feel the pressure of the roots releasing themselves into sprouts. Only the walnut tree is still waiting.

I cut the lawn with the scythe. I sharpen it, cut, sharpen. The quick swishing of the blade is a short breath.

I like mowing by hand, the stroke from right to left that levels the grass comes to me easily.

Today I feel less like doing work and more like keeping myself busy with work, depending on it to make the hours go by.

The cut grass releases its scent to the sun. I gather it with a rake.

At the gate Selim is cheerful about the warmth and has a new shirt on. "It's spring, man, you need to wear something new."

He's tall and robust, a tree-trunk of a man. He has the money and wants to buy me the promised bottle.

"At noon I have to go somewhere, I'm not going to the tavern," I tell him.

"I'm coming with you," he says.

"It would be better if you didn't, Selim."

"It would be better if I did, man."

He says it with such assurance that I shut up.

He helps me to pile up the cuttings then we chew sardines and bread together in the April air.

"Grass is good for animals," he says. "Mine would have

a party with this, a shame to throw it away. My animals are thin but healthy. In a little while they'll be putting down children and I have to be there."

I say nothing about the place I'm looking for. He asks nothing.

We go about like two laborers taking a walk on their lunch hour. He gnaws and gnaws on his olive pit.

At the entrance I recognize the car from that morning. We stop to get a good look at it. I enter the small lane that leads to the gate then I return. It's a new building, not many names on the buzzers.

It's all residences on the street, only one flower stand.

Selim looks around with his nose in the air, as if he senses rain.

We're two laborers who have come about a job, we don't know the exact address. No one walks by, just two elderly people on a stroll, each with a dog.

We circle behind the building. I want to see the sides. I don't know what to try, but I know that my nerves will teach me on the spot.

We go back without speaking. Selim measures his steps, doesn't hurry them. He presses his feet on the ground and lifts them a little more than necessary.

He's already treading his own lands and leading his herd, I think. He gnaws and sucks at an olive pit.

In the garden I start mowing again.

Selim cuts the lavender beds. Then he prepares bouquets with a string, sitting on the ground with his legs crossed.

"Your garden is giving me business."

From one pocket he takes out his knife, a strong blade more experienced than my scythe. He piles up bouquets to dry.

Without calling my attention I feel as if he is speaking in my direction, but with his eyes on his hands. "You don't want my money, you don't want the wine for my debt. That's how you keep someone tied to you, not set him free. You say no to a man and don't give him the peace of repayment. I have to honor my pledge. You have to be friends with men and you have to be even."

I hear him spitting out the olive pit.

I keep working. His words are meant to be understood without the indiscretion of turning toward him.

From the lawn's edge Selim's voice interrupts me when the hours are done. He is saying good-bye. I hold my arm out for his hand. He widens his hands and places them on my shoulders. He gives me a toothy, wide-open smile, and hugs me.

His departure is decided. This is our farewell.

There is a bitter pang in my mouth and I feel bad about the promised wine that I don't allow him to pour.

"The time for wine is over, man. I'm taking away the last bundle of my debt. I will repay you all at once." And he gives a remote, ancient smile, a breath of Africa, a grain of pollen dropped by the scirocco wind on its journey, a migrating beehive, a whiteness of wings in his mouth that subsides.

He goes to the gate with a bundle of lavender under his arm.

Then I close my eyes behind the back of my hand, against the lost pieces of a single day, and do something stupid. I get down on my knees on the grass and comb through it, search, find the smooth olive pit and plant it in a pot with dark soil.

I should go home and sleep on it then put my hands back in my pockets like before Laila. I knew the evil of killing before her so I can spare her the trouble. I'll go. I have to be quick. There's nothing to prepare. I'll go and pull it off tonight, like Argentina.

All the while my nerves grow tougher. I think I can attack him, knock him down. If he's carrying a gun he'll use it, if not I'll manage.

I feel a reckless force rising from the mouth of my stomach. There's a calm in my head, which is steadier than it used to be. Argentina doesn't leave your body. A little skin grows over the ulcer of war and assassins.

And a woman arrives who at first sight knows who I am and isn't repelled, but she chooses me and sticks me back in the pigeonhole of infamy.

This time I don't run away, this time I stay.

I bring gloves along.

It's still light when I leave by the gate, so I can drop by to chat with the tavern-keeper. He's decanting wine, I give him a hand. Then he frees a table from the chairs on top and brings me a little bit of goat cheese, some dark bread and a carafe of red. He talks about a house by the sea where he wants to retire.

"Me too," I say, thinking of a house along the coast, a window to the East and a pergola to the South. "For me the West and North belong at my back."

"For me," he says, "the West is my father's back when he leaves for the Americas. I can still see him boarding the ship and disappearing into the West, forever."

"Our lives are no longer that way. Now we have the lives of other people who come to us at any point except a port. Strange, isn't it? Even people carrying a passport don't go through a port."

"That's why at my place there's always a spot and a plate for those lives."

I chew something and take a couple of sips of wine. The evening is ready and I have to get up.

He asks if I'm going home. "No, I'm not going."

I don't know how my reply sounds. The tavern-keeper shakes my hand and with his other hand he touches my arm, which is already tense and bitter.

The road is far, I need to walk it, get my footsteps and blood moving at the same pace.

I listen to my breathing, to my heartbeat.

I calm and harden myself.

In my arms I feel a crushing force, enough to knock the bottom out of a barrel.

On the street I brush by people that come toward me. I'm afraid of bumping into someone and already causing injury this way.

I cross paths with a woman, change sidewalks before she does. A murderer has to be in a void.

I walk and my body gears up.

I take heavier steps. My arms accompany my pace by moving very little, absorbed in this waiting to go off.

My hands hold my fingers outstretched, separate, to keep them from brushing against each other.

The air feels light around my lower legs.

From the edge of my nails and the tips of my hair comes a constant checking of the barbed-wire fence between myself and the world.

My eyes see inside, too. They stare at my heart and its slow, dense beatings. They scan my spinal cord, the stiffened snake inside each man's skeleton that gives us the erect posture of a reptile about to strike.

And now I know I'm a man because I am the most dangerous animal.

This is not a hunt. It's an act of destruction.

When this feeling comes to me, I am ready.

So many soldiers fall when they don't make it to this point.

I was born under the sky of Taurus. Through my nostrils you can easily insert a ring to drag me around.

I come to the corner of the street and see a little movement, a cluster of people under a lamp. An accident, I think, and start to walk and the crowd is right at the number that I had checked at noon. And I see policemen and a barrier and I end up pressed against it and a guy in uniform asks me to walk around since I can't go through there. I ask what's happening and he hurries me along brusquely with a hand gesture. The gate that I have to walk by is the one with the turmoil. And I've been ready for a whole carload of time and I'd even walk on top of them and throw myself on the man and now my arm is tensed like a bow, like a hammer, and I could shoot a hole in the ground if I pointed down. And I can't just put it in my pocket and go back.

I suddenly turn and think of climbing over that part of the wall and I take two steps and feel a breath of sulfur released by my nose and heat coming out and dripping down my face and I realize that it's blood. My nostrils are gushing spurts of it on the ground with the beating of my arteries. A man offers me a handkerchief and tells me to hold my head back and I obey and close my eyes and hear a woman's voice talking about a black man and I think of Selim with his nice new shirt and I lean against a wall and sit down and maybe I sleep.

I open my eyes to the voice of the man with the handkerchief and I don't know what I'm doing sitting on a sidewalk, leaning against a wall with people around me.

I see blood on my fingers, feel it spread on my face and my strength coming back.

I pull myself to my feet, thank him for the kindness. The group moves away and the man with the handkerchief touches my arm for support. I notice it's empty, slow, discharged, and I remember.

The man invites me to come in to clean myself off. He's a doctor and has a walk-in clinic next door. He wants to take my blood pressure.

He asks me things, my job, where, I answer.

He apologizes for speaking, for meddling, but it helps him to check the reflexes and the nervous responses.

I can wash myself at his place. In the mirror I'm a red clown with smudges everywhere.

I wash, rub, and can't explain an underlying feeling of happiness. The deed decided still has to be done and the wasted time is closing in on Laila. What's more, my face is known on this street and it'll be harder to come out unharmed. But the lost blood gives me relief.

I come out of the bathroom feeling more confident. The man has the nice brown bony face of a Southern peasant, fine skin over his bones, like unleavened bread.

A head of thick white hair.

While he fumbles around with my arm he tells me that he's retiring to his hometown, a place that reminds me of a wine. I realize I only meet people about to leave.

He's renovating a house and a farm. He wants to set his feet on the ground.

He doesn't want any more city, any more people with horrible wounds, bullets, drugs, nerves. He wants to treat bones, hearts, old people.

My blood pressure is fine, he advises a glass of wine. Then he thinks of the man over whom he was bent before me and tells me that they killed him the old way, like a field animal, slitting his throat.

Someone, a woman, sees a black man grab a man getting out of the car and cut his throat. And she sees him go away without even a spatter of blood on his shirt.

He runs to the cries in the street, finds a woman shaking with fear and on the ground is a puddle of blood, and not far away is a man stretched out, face down.

He takes his pulse to be on the safe side and goes back in to get a towel to cover at least the face.

"A man dies and his skin loses heat like the sand on a summer evening. It makes you feel like warming him up," he says.

"He must have almost not noticed. The cut is deep, not jagged, from a very sharp blade. He must have only felt a chill."

And then along comes me, as if there isn't enough blood on the street, I add mine, too.

He listens to my chest with the cold ear of an instrument.

While he measures the beats I come to understand Selim's ashes, his good-bye. I can't hold back what I understand. The lost blood makes me empty.

The man says my heart muscle is as big as a coconut. At the end he breaks away from the listening.

We leave each other cordially, I thank him, he tells me that he will come by to ask for advice about soil and tools.

I turn my back on the place of the blood.

I go to the station, to a train that sends me back home.

To return, a verb that drives me. I return from the South of an Argentinian hour. I sail the hundred parallels in a night, separate from Laila. I don't want to think about the friend who redeems a debt with an embrace and a slit throat.

I forbid his name. Just thinking it is a betrayal.

I turn toward the point in the fields where Africa should be.

I stand facing it with my eyes closed, like the blind when they turn toward smiles they can hear.

I have to return, sit in the kitchen, replace blood with wine.

I sit at the window of a train. There are no workers at this hour of the evening, just students and shopgirls.

They return, later than us.

I look at them, they have an urge to laugh with each other, to be cheerful in the little that remains of the day.

They laugh in gales that carry them away, they laugh the way I walk, the way I drink.

I touch the book in my pocket. This will take care of a good stretch of the return. I leave it alone, convalescence for future days.

I touch the spot where the bullet passed without taking me along.

The girls prepare to get off. I follow last.

On the sidewalk I raise my nose to the sky and smell the odor of my dried blood.

There are evenings when the sky is an egg and you can look at it from inside.

A northwest wind carries rust and salt. Iron gets sick here but the basil thrives handsomely.

From the landing I hear its welcome.

I set the table with something, turn off the light, sit down.

I chew in the dark, absorb, listen, swallow.

It's a clear night, moonless. I scent my fingers with parsley and garlic, a little oil from the bread drips into my palm and I'm happy to be anointed by oil and not blood.

I pass the back of my hand over my brow to wipe away the day.

I'm not innocent. This isn't relief. It's just the physical release of a nasal menses.

Another man takes my place as a murderer. He removes not the guilt but the gesture. Now his arm bears a replica of the blow to a throat.

And his arm contracts to vacantly repeat the shape of a gesture until only a hint is left.

An athlete prepares his event though many practices, to train himself. A murderer repeats the movement of death afterward, in his nerves, till he has exhausted it, to tear it off through a reverse training.

I know that he is taking the knife with him to keep cutting bread, making flower bouquets and splitting fruit.

Whoever knows things and the value of using them never abandons them to a last cursed service.

In the darkness of the kitchen my second horse dies.

The people of a year migrate in a day, no more hold-me's or olive pits.

I stay behind. At least tonight I don't touch the emptiness they have left.

I fall asleep at the table and wake a little before dawn.

I have to retrain myself to days without opening my mouth.

I take the book stopped at a fold, deliver myself to its pace, to the breathing of the other storyteller. If I am someone else, it's also because books move men more than journeys and years.

After many pages you end up learning a variant, a different move than the one taken and thought inevitable.

I break away from what I am when I learn to treat my own life differently.

In dim light I shave my damp face and the razor tries to cross my skin in another direction.

I put the book in my jacket's inside pocket. I point it toward my chest. Where the gun used to be, now there is its opposite.

When Erri De Luca published his first novel, *Non ora, non qui* (Not here, not now) in 1989, he became a young writer at the age of 39. The story he told evoked not only his own youth but also the collective, mythic youth of modern Italy, born on the ruins of the Second World War. A boy comes of age in 1950s Naples, going to school and playing along the docks with the hardscrabble children of the poor. The son of a middle-class family fallen on hard times, he is torn between the exuberance and noise of the streets and the orderly stillness of his home life. When his family's fortunes improve, the narrator experiences it not as a welcome improvement but as an irremediable loss.

Told entirely in the first person, this aging son's confession to his estranged mother revisits the archetypal scene of Italian neorealism: the poverty and devastation of southern Italy during and immediately after the war. As emblems of pathos and symbols of hope for a better future, children figure prominently in these circumstances. Nowhere is this more evident than in cinematic masterpieces of the 1940s, from the child partisans in *Open City* to the street children of *Paisà* and the doggedly loyal son in *The Bicycle Thief.* Unlike these resourceful and sometimes heroic children, however, De Luca's protagonist has his gaze set on a past that he can only recall through a veil of nostalgia and re-gret. The story he relates is not an external chronicle of survival but rather an interior monologue of surrender, punctuated by fragmentary glimpses of the outside world. The narrator remembers his childhood as a quiet, lonely time, when he suffered from a bad stutter that only came "untangled" when he discovered writing: "Speaking is like walking on a string. Writing, instead, is possessing it, wind-ing it into a ball."[1]

De Luca wrote like a man returning from a long exile, breaking his silence in a trickle of spare, carefully pondered words. He was hailed by Raffaele La Capria, a fellow Nea-politan writer from the fabled postwar generation, for "A tone of voice that is unmistakable at first grasp, an integ-rity of vision that lends the right focus to thoughts and feelings."[2] *Non ora, non qui*, like De Luca's subsequent works, is relentlessly autobiographical. The author has ad-mitted to being able to write only of things experienced directly, hence his consistent use of first-person narrative. As he has said in an interview with Silvio Perrella, "Writ-ing is an attempt to create a definitive version—shorter, more brusque and abusive—of the life you've lived: Ar-

---

1. Erri De Luca, *Non ora, non qui* (Milan: Feltrinelli, 1989), p. 25.
2. *Ibid.*, back cover.

rested, detained for a spell, fixed inside a container that prevents it from aging."[3]

The historical context in which De Luca emerged as a writer lends a sense of urgency to his words, and casts a veil of nostalgia over his vision. The 1990s was a decade ushered in by a major break with the past. After the unraveling of the Soviet Union in the late 1980s, it no longer made much sense to contrast Western-style capitalism with a functional model of communism. Marxism and its political embodiment in Moscow and Beijing had long been a beacon for Italian writers of the left, who were the dominant force in postwar Italian culture. Consequently, the collapse of Soviet communism and the death of ideology, as it has been called, left many of them adrift. Not only did the battle lines have to be redrawn: the entire map had to be thrown out.

In Italy, political and cultural discourse have long been intertwined. Artists and writers are expected to comment on public life through columns in the major newspapers, speeches at protest rallies, or even the holding of elective

---

3. Silvio Perrella, "Erri De Luca: Voci di un vocabulario. Un dialogo." Recorded interview, http://www.feltrinelli.it/IntervistaInterna?id_int=1331.

office. Italy has rewarded some of its most prominent men of culture an appointment as senator-for-life (most recently to the poet Mario Luzi). Not everyone in Italy agrees, of course, that the artist or the artwork must necessarily be an instrument of social change. Such a notion was adamantly rejected, in particular, by the neo-avantgarde of the 1960s, out of which grew the postmodernism best known through the novels of Italo Calvino and Umberto Eco. Eco, in particular, helped to create a vogue for erudite disquisition that has been given new impetus today in the works of Roberto Calasso and Guido Ceronetti.

The world of letters was not immune to the calls for change that rocked Italian politics and society in the 1990s. One of the most refreshing innovations to emerge was freer experimentation with prose. Literary Italian has always been quite forbidding to its acolytes, representing an ideal literary standard rather than an idiom that the majority of people actually speak. Young writers came increasingly to reject the imposition this represented, in favor of a medium that more closely resembled colloquial patterns of speech and the variations in dialect that distinguish one region from the other.

In this postmodern climate, Erri De Luca was almost an anachronism, more reminiscent of the politically engaged artists of the postwar era than of the new writers. While he is indeed one of the great innovators of contemporary Italian prose, his allegiance to the recent past, both as a writer and as a political activist, places him in a class by himself. He belongs to the generation that had consumed its youth in the political turmoil of 1968, which he has called "the century's most imprisoned generation." Unlike the many who have abjured the experience of those years, De Luca makes no apologies about his active participation in the extreme left-wing movements of the '60s and '70s. In fact, he places them at the front and center of his curriculum vitae and of his aesthetic creed.

As the historian Paul Ginsborg describes it: "The Italian protest movement was the most profound and long-lasting in Europe. It spread from the schools and universities into the factories, and then out again into the society as a whole."[4] What had started out as a protest against working conditions at the Fiat factory in Turin in 1969 turned into a nationwide political movement calling for revolutionary change. One of the largest and most charismatic of the various radical factions was "Lotta Continua" (Ongoing Struggle), a coalition of workers and students that grew out of the Fiat assemblies. It would last, growing in influence and militancy, until 1976, when it splintered after the defeat of the Italian Communist Party at the

---

4. Paul Ginsborg, *A History of Contemporary: Society and Politics, 1943-1988* (Harmondsworth: Penguin, 1989), p. 298.

general elections. For De Luca, who describes himself as one of the leaders of Lotta Continua, the story ends in 1980, when the Fiat management announced thousands of layoffs and broke the back of organized labor. He describes this moment in his short story collection, *In alto a sinistra* (Above, to the left): "In a single night the great factory had gotten rid of twenty-four thousand meals in the cafeteria, and forty-eight thousand hands, perhaps fewer, since people injured on the job were also among the expelled. 'Go outside to eat,' they said. And outside we would stay for forty days and forty nights, by fires to keep us warm. No one exited, no one entered the factory we were blockading. In the end we would all remain outside: friends, strangers, defeated."[5]

In its most extreme form, the militancy of the 1970s led to the political assassination of persons who had been deemed enemies of the revolution. So pervasive was the general atmosphere of violence that the decade is remembered in Italian annals as "The Years of Lead." De Luca makes no attempt to justify the taking of human life, but he is clearly reluctant to tailor a response for those who would automatically criticize those deeds today. His stance is recorded elliptically in *Aceto, arcobaleno* (Vinegar, rain-

---

5. Erri De Luca, "Conversazione di fianco," in *In alto a sinistra* (Milan: Feltrinelli, 1994), p. 77.

bow), where an assassin admits the senselessness of his crimes but adds, "I do not wish to reconstruct the motives for a death sentence against an enemy. I remove that act from any contour that might accommodate it. Instead I speak of its consequences on me."[6]

In the same collection, which forms a fascinating companion piece to *Three Horses*, De Luca gives a trenchant portrait of the era: "In those years no one wanted to be light. A different gravity impelled that changed the pace of many. When it ended, everyone went about erasing it, putting on sneakers."[7] Once the age of protest was over, De Luca went into an exile of sorts, on the margins of society, his class, and his country, choosing to work as a truck driver, day laborer, and mason in Africa and France. He has called this period a time of "slowness," when amid the grinding rhythms of manual labor and the silence of the long days, he discovered his dimension as a writer: "It was the just rhythm of heavy labor and its gestures, but it was also a time without revolt in which I felt like a foreigner. In the slowness I learned ancient Hebrew, the language of origin of the Sacred Scriptures, and about the mountains, as a rock climber."[8] Translating the Hebrew Bible and

6. Erri De Luca, *Aceto, arcobaleno* (Milan: Feltrinelli, 1992), p. 33.

7. *Ibid.*, 20.

8. Erri De Luca. "I tempi della vita," http://www.educational. rai.it/railibro/intervise .asp?id=118.

mountain climbing—two of De Luca's greatest passions—
may be strange bedfellows, but they are emblematic of the
search for origins and fearlessness that animates his writing.

It is against this backdrop of political activism, disil-
lusionment, and exile that the story told in *Three Horses*
evolves. The battleground shifts from 1970s Italy to the
Argentina of the Dirty War and the thousands of *des-
aparecidos* who never received a burial. The title is derived
from a nursery rhyme recited in the mountains of the
Emilia region: "*Tre anni una siepe, tre siepi un cane, tre cani
un cavallo, tre cavalli un uomo.*" In three years a hedge, three
hedges a dog, three dogs a horse, three horses a man. According to this measure, a man's life lasts as long as that
of three horses: twenty-seven times three. Somewhere in
Calabria, on the southernmost tip of Italy's eastern shore-
line, a middle-aged man spends his days in solitude, tending a garden, reading used books, and struggling not to
remember. He is already on his second life, the first having been extinguished on the plains of Patagonia, during
his flight from the military authorities who had murdered
his young wife. A woman enters his life, and as he falls in
love the memories of this earlier time come flooding back.
At the same time he makes a new friend, a migrant worker
from Africa, bearing the ancient wisdom of another continent. By the end of the novel the narrator's second life,

too, will have ended, but in the empty space it leaves behind, something new will grow.

One of the underlying themes of De Luca's works is the redemptive power of memory, his embrace of it being perhaps the main feature that he shares with other writers of his generation. This theme burns into the pages of *Three Horses*, where from the start the narrator makes known his preference for used books, since the pages stay in place after you've turned them. The narrator's relationship to the past is fraught, a difficulty he expresses by telling the entire story, including the many flashbacks to his Argentinean years, in the present tense. When his lover, Laila, probes him about this usage, he replies enigmatically. "What do I want with verbal gymnastics? I am not the master of time. I'm its beast of burden."

The eternal present of *Three Horses* is only the most prominent of its many stylistic peculiarities. In this, the most poetic and experimental of De Luca's novels, the author has distilled the turbulent matter of his earlier stories into a prose that is rigorously stripped down, essential and concrete. Even basic references to organic functions are replaced by their most material equivalents. There is no eating or drinking in his vocabulary. There is only chewing or swallowing. To dance is to "tap your feet." To exhale is to "expel air from the nostrils."

Here one feels the weight of De Luca's long apprenticeship as a translator of the Hebrew Bible. Many aspects of his prose are reminiscent of features typical of Biblical prose.[9] De Luca operates within a narrow, concrete vocabulary, repeating words, almost obsessively, to amplify their richness and meaning rather than drawing on synonyms. *Terra*, *premura*, and *mossa* are frequent visitors to these pages, creating no small amount of difficulty for translation into English. *Terra*, for instance, means "earth," "ground," "land," and "soil." How to choose one word that will render both the metaphysical perspective and the feelings of a gardener crumbling dirt between his fingers?

The same influence comes to bear on the syntax. Sentences string along in parallel structures, with the conjunction "and" appearing at the beginning and at repeated intervals in the middle. More sophisticated conjunctions such as "although," "despite" or even "since" are implicitly rejected, as if De Luca wished to strip his prose of the accretions of literary history. His sentences often consist of a series of run-on phrases, held together by serial commas and perhaps, but not always, a common subject. These usages have been slightly attenuated in the English, in order to capture the rhythm of the original.

---

9. For a concise description of the style of biblical Hebrew, see Robert Alter's "To the Reader" in his translation and commentary of *Genesis* (New York: Norton, 1996), pp. ix–xlvii.

It is in the area of style that De Luca steps outside of his normally content-driven aesthetic to engage in what critics call metalinguistics, or language commenting on itself. He has often said that Italian is really his father tongue, quite literally, the language spoken by his father, and by inference, the language of the books in his father's study. In *Montedidio* (*God's Mountain*), his most successful novel both commercially and critically, the young narrator remarks, "I write in Italian because it is quiet, and into it I can put the events of the day, sheltered from the noise of Neapolitan."[10] The Neapolitan dialect, instead, is his mother tongue, the language spoken to him by his mother, and the language of the streets of his childhood.

De Luca continues to experiment and explore in his works, most recently by writing a play in dialect (*Morso di una luna nuova*), but he remains true to the ideals of his youth. His methods may have changed and his voice become more limpid, more articulate, but he still advocates, now as before, a stubborn resistance. The new target of his protest is no longer solely capitalism and consumerism. It is a broader, more metaphysical quest to restore a human dimension to our lives, and reclaim the earthly rhythms of nature for ourselves. His admonition was already clear

---

10. Erri De Luca, *God's Mountain*, trans. by Michael F. Moore (New York: Riverhead Books, 2002).

in his first novel, *Non ora, non qui:* "If we move constantly, we give a sense, a direction to time. But if we stop, digging in our heels like a donkey in the middle of the trail, if we let ourselves be carried away by daydreams, then time stops and is no longer a burden that weighs on our backs. If we refuse to carry it, it pours out, spilling about like the ink stain that my pen makes balanced upright on the blotter, then falling over, empty."[11]

Michael F. Moore
New York, March 2005

---

11. *Non ora, non qui*, p. 44.

Selected works by Erri De Luca

NOVELS
Non ora, non qui
Tu, mio (*Sea of Memory*, trans. Beth Archer Brombert)
Montedidio (*God's Mountain*, trans. Michael Moore)

SHORT STORIES
Aceto, arcobaleno
In alto a sinistra
Il contrario di uno

POETRY
Opera sull'acqua e altre poesie

PLAYS
L'ultimo viaggio di Sinbad
Morso di una luna nuova

TRANSLATIONS FROM THE BIBLE
Esodo / Nomi
Giona / Ionà
Kohèlet / Ecclesiaste
Libro di Rut